THE SECOND
TIJUANA BIBLE READER

THE SECOND TIJUANA BIBLE READER

AN ANTHOLOGY OF CLASSIC GAY STORIES

VICTOR J. BANIS, EDITOR

THE BORGO PRESS

MMXII

THE SECOND TIJUANA BIBLE READER

SECOND BORGO PRESS EDITION

Published by Wildside Press LLC

www.wildsidebooks.com

DEDICATION

I am deeply indebted to my friend, Heather, for all the help she has given me in getting these early works of mine reissued.

And I am grateful as well to Rob Reginald, for all his assistance and support.

CONTENTS

FOREWORD

Contrary to what many people may think, the writing of what is crassly referred to as "smut stories" and/or "Tijuana Bibles" is not exactly a talentless occupation. Not everyone is gifted enough to sit down and turn out a pornographic short story. It requires a knack for hard-hitting, action-packed description and dialogue. If the sexual episode is too detailed or, on the other hand, is not detailed enough, the story will prove disappointing to the purchaser and reader. The author must concentrate on appeasing his readers' sexual appetites by luring him into an inescapable sex-trap. This can only be accomplished by the gradual building up of sexual suspense and heated anticipation. The approach to the sexual sex experience must be enticing—not too lengthy. It must excite and arouse the reader; it must titillate and stimulate him. A truly successful story will stimulate the solitary reader to such a point that he or she will masturbate themselves to orgasm before they finish reading the story to its end.

Characterization, grammar, correct word usage, spelling punctuation, etc., are unimportant in the erotic short story. The characters need only be described physically and their attitudes, personalities, social backgrounds, are usually never included except, of course in instances where it is necessary that the reader be told that the hero is a masochist or a sadist and that the female lead is a Lesbian or a nymphomaniac, etc. It requires a definite skill to write a successful erotic short story.

Stories such as are contained in this volume are geared to

the young, both in mind and body, and, strangely enough, they seem to enjoy a great deal of appeal amongst the more intellectual of our society. This contention was borne out by Dr. Alfred Kinsey in his *Sexual Behavior in the Human Male*, wherein he asserted that the higher degree of intelligence and the greater amount of education seems to cause an attraction toward hardcore pornography. The psychology behind this line of reasoning is that the highly intelligent individual resorts to pornography because there is no hidden meaning, no mental exertion needed to comprehend the author's intent. The language is simple, strong and direct. The highly educated person is given a chance to relax and read for the pure and simple pleasure of reading. Another school of thought is that the highly educated individual is not as sexually concentrated as the individual of lower intelligence. The intellectual does not have as keen an interest in sex as does his less educated cousin. He resorts to pornography because it acts as a stimulant and gratifies the minor sex urges that are necessary to make him qualify as being human without the necessity of having to involve himself with a partner or people.

Although the stories in this collection are homosexually oriented, this does not mean to imply that all such "Tijuana Bibles" are written for the homosexual market. On the contrary, the majority of this type short story is usually heterosexual in nature. The original stories were written to be sold outside the United States to servicemen and tourists who were interested in obtaining such illegal items as hard-core-pornographic-stories. What traveler in Paris does not seek out the famous "dirty post card"? What tourist in Hamburg does not visit the Reeperbahn in order to see for himself the underground establishments that stage sex exhibitions and similar entertainment (although there they are not entirely underground). What red-blooded American male would refuse to attend a stag party for a friend where the inevitable "dirty movies" are shown to the guests. The appeal of sex is one which cannot be driven out of man. The instincts of the human being are geared toward sex, either consciously or subconsciously and it is only the narrow-minded, the badly educated, the Victorian thinking individuals who refuse to accept life as it is and who condemn and chastise all matters dealing with sexual functions and relationships.

Drs. Eberhard and Phyllis Kronhausen co-authored a book entitled *Pornography And The Law (The Psychology of Erotic Realism and Hard Core Pornography)*. Drs. Kronhausen were attending hearings of a California State Legislative committee on pornography in the fall of 1958. A young police officer testified that a certain picture on the cover of a certain brochure was obscene because it depicted the female genitalia quite clearly. One of the authors of the brochure, a female, resented the idea that any part of the female anatomy should be considered as being obscene. It was contended that if any part of the human body, male or female, is indecent, lewd, and obscene, then the whole human body is indecent, lewd, and obscene. And, if this be the case and the human body is considered to be indecent, lewd, and obscene, then life is obscene and the whole creation is in one hell of a sorry state of affairs. The same test may be applied to literature, art, and other forms of artistic expression.

Morals, like manners, differ with each culture (as well as with each individual). Here in the United States a certain prominent metropolitan museum of art was restrained by the postal authorities from mailing out prints of a certain famous nude painting. Yet, at the very same time in one of the major foreign nations of the world this same identical painting was being reproduced for use on the country's new postage stamp.

So, who is to say what is obscene and what is not? America may set the trends for economic, political, and industrial progress, but we cannot set ourselves up as judges and dictators insofar as the matters of morals are concerned. Some cultures look upon Americans as barbaric because we believe in monogamy and (until quite recently) would not practice birth control. Because of eugenics and infanticide we cannot say that the moral codes of the Asian or the African are wrong simply because they do not correspond with our own. R.E.L. Masters advised that we should always keep in mind the vast differences between the values and customs of Africa and the East from those of the West. Slavery is still to be found in many places; harems continue to exist; polygamy is supplemented by concubinage, and in India, one of the most ancient of all human institutions, that of sacred temple prostitution, still flourishes despite all efforts to suppress it. There was a time when man's sexual necessities were sated without having to go "underground". There is every reason to believe that such a time will come again. Man must function as he was intended to function and the suppression of his natural urges and instincts will only result in mental and/or physical collapse and decay.

The "Tijuana Bible" short story is another implement used by many to help relieve the pressures and the frustrations which an anti-sex culture creates for the normal individual. Because the language is not what is generally considered "polite", "refined", literary achievement.

Suppose, for instance, that when the English language was being developed that the word "inspire" was decided to be classified amongst the list of obscene and socially objectionable words. If such had been the case, then today we would go to any extreme to avoid using the word "inspire" in our conversation. But, "inspire" is NOT a dirty word; however, the word "fuck" is, yet "fuck" is merely a slang derivation of "fornicate"; as "inspire" evolves from "spiritual". The question that remains to be asked is: who has decided which words are obscene and which words are not; and, whomsoever did make such decisions then is it not about time that we realized that they have been dead these many centuries and it is about time our modern thinkers revised that antiquated word plan?

An amusing incident took place within the last several years which involved the use of the word "horn". It seems that an American film company released a movie for universal distribution which they entitled *Young Man with a Horn*. When the movie was shown in London the various marquees of the theaters showing the film read: *Young Man of Music*. It seems that the word "horn" in Merry Old English slang refers to a man's erect penis.

It is the thought behind the word and the individual interpretation placed upon it that makes the real difference; it is not the word itself that is at fault. Therefore, the words found in the stories in this collection are not placed there to shock the reader, but are included in the story in order to create a bridge between author, reader, and character(s). The (what is considered by some to be) strong language puts the reader at ease because he is at home with himself, so to speak. The social niceties which are expected of him are removed and he can relax and lose himself to his fantasies. Whether the characters in the stories are female or male makes little difference. If they speak with a hard hitting, plain, coarse, direct tongue, the reader finds the kind of persons he wants to know at that particular time. When this same reader has lost his desire for sexual outlet, or has experienced an orgasm as a result of reading a "Tijuana Bible," chances are, when he glances again at the erotic short story, he may feel a twinge of resentment, disappointment, even disgust—although moments before he had devoured every word of that story with a ravenous sexual appetite.

There are several theories set forth as to why the erotic story enjoys continuous popularity. Dr. Douglas H. Gamlin stated that one reason is that stories such as this deal with an interpersonal relationship. Dr. Gamlin claims that this is important because as our world grows larger and communications become more and more sophisticated, the world community shrinks and so does the circle of man's friends; the more sophisticated the world community becomes, the more impersonal life in that community must be. Yet the normal individual has a driving need to be involved and the more impersonal life around him becomes, the stronger that need becomes. Being that love and friendship are important factors in our lives, and even if we fear becoming involved ourselves, we do enjoy reading about others who do become involved. Stripping away the so-called obscene words and the sex scenes, these stories boil down to nothing but pure and simple love stories. Look closely and you will find a story about lonely people in an impersonal world who are grasping at a human relationship, be it heterosexual or homosexual.

The people who enjoy reading such literature as is herein contained very often receive a thrill from vicariously participating in the experiences of the story's character or characters. The reader may never hope to realize similar experiences in his lifetime and may be fully aware that such experiences are purely figments of an authors imagination, but still he likes to escape from reality and lose himself in the erotic world of make believe, surrounding himself with these fictional sex seekers and doers.

But whatever theory lies behind an individual's reason for turning to the "Tijuana Bibles" for sexual release, the fact remains that they do enjoy universal appeal and should be read not as pieces of "trashy literature" but as a representation of a form of literary art which has, since the beginning of communication by written word, occupied a unique niche in our existence.

PART ONE

THERE'S ALWAYS A FIRST TIME FOR EVERYTHING

A young man's first sexual experience is generally masturbation, either privately or with a buddy or group of friends; and these first sex experiences are usually homosexual. Mutual masturbation is extremely common in the early teen years of the adolescent boy. Many youngsters never graduate from this homosexual phase of their growth. Many appear to grow out of this phase but subconsciously harbor the desire to relive these early homosexual experiences well after they have married and have sired children. Men such as these are considered to be "latent homosexuals."

Although arguments continue as to the cause of homosexuality, some psychiatrists and psychologists believe that homosexuality is innate, others think that is acquired. Our first sex experiences are very often something that we carry with us until our dying day. How often have you thought about the first time you ever had sex with another person? It is generally found that the mature, firmly entrenched heterosexual male hardly ever admits, even to himself, a first sex experience if it was with another male (and chances are that it was). He would, of course, drive such homosexual experiences from his mind, fearing that recognition of such perverse behavior would only shake the foundations of his confirmed heterosexuality.

The two stories that follow, "Straight Pick Up" and "Two Boys and a Teacher," were very obviously written by an overt homosexual. The plots are perversely romantic and the endings are the sort of thing a homosexual might dream about. In the first story, "Straight Pick Up" the handsome young Marine is easily lured into overt homosexual practices. He exhibits no doubts, no qualms, no fears. He happily performs oral/genital acts for the very first time with a veritable stranger. The story is absolutely idyllic and the type of experience every homosexual male wishes for. It is considered to be good escape fiction.

In the second story, "Two Boys and a Teacher," the reader becomes aware that the boys' first sex experiences took place prior to the story's beginning. The boys have obviously had many sex sessions together and coitus with a female teacher was something they had never experienced. Again this story must have been penned by an overt homosexual. In reading it you will note the explicit detail paid to all of the males in the story—the poor female teacher is practically forgotten in the last scenes. Even when the boys lure the young lady to the cabin and she is surrounded by eight sex-starved young men, the narrator proceeds to focus all attention on the homosexual acts rather than on the heterosexual. Like all "Tijuana Bible" stories, the endings are happy and perfect. The lonely characters have found their excitement and have also found a future for themselves.

Pause and think back on your first sex experiences. When you have vividly recalled them to mind, read "Straight Pick-up" and "Two Boys and a Teacher." Perhaps your introduction to sexual relations were along similar lines.

CHAPTER ONE
STRAIGHT PICK-UP

I was standing on the corner, waiting for the light to change, when I saw him standing there listening to one of the numerous preachers cluttering the corner. He was about five foot six or seven and weighed about one-hundred and forty-five pounds. His hair was dark and cut very short and contrasted beautifully with his blue eyes. Judging from his clothes: gray continentals, not too tight, and a blue striped shirt, I supposed he was in the service personnel, no matter what they are wearing, that stands out.

It is sort of a neatness or cleanness that you see nowhere else. The light turned green, but I hesitated and then I walked over to listen to the preacher. I stood right behind the guy and made some comment about the ridiculousness of the spiel that we were listening to. He smiled politely and agreed. His smile was beautiful. I hurried to continue the conversation and he seemed agreeable. We talked for a few moments and he seemed so at ease that I was encouraged to suggest a cup of coffee. He hesitated a moment and then agreed. Of course, when I had first seen him, my immediate thoughts were of sex, but the more I talked to him, the more he seemed so off guard to anything like this, so unaware of his good looks, that I decided not to try to make him.

He was so good looking though, that I had to stay with him as long as possible anyway. We went to a coffee shop just up the street and sat at a table in the back. The waitress brought the coffee and I put some money in the juke box. To the background of Earl Grant's *Malagueña,* I discovered his name was Alan. It fit; I offered him a cigarette and lit it for him. It was refreshing not to have him hold my hand as I did so. For some reason, if he had, I would have been very disappointed. As he drank his coffee, I looked at his hands. They were not too large, like the rest of him, and they were finely masculine. I noticed that his nails were clean.

He told me that he had been up all the night before at a wedding reception for one of his buddies. Consequently, he was very tired. We had discussed going to a movie, but after hearing this, we decided against it. He was so friendly and natural, I still couldn't believe it. I hadn't used any of my usual tactics to get him up to my room, and yet I felt that if I asked him to come up, that he would agree.

It was as simple as that. No big story to get him up there, no falseness about it at all. I just asked him and he said, yes. We left the cafe and walked to my hotel. I was very calm, and felt at ease with him. We went up to my room. He lay down on his back on the bed and sighed and stretched. I turned on the radio and he picked up my copy of *Catcher in the Rye.* I had just finished reading it and it was lying on the nightstand. He thumbed through it and we talked about it a little bit. I felt so strange being here like this. Everything was so natural. I couldn't keep my eyes off him, but he seemed unaware of it. I suddenly remembered that I hadn't found out what branch of the service he was in. I still assumed that he was in one of them. He said that he was in the Marines and I almost fell over. This was like no Marine I had ever met before. Conversation lagged after this and it was obvious that before long he was going to be asleep. I reached over and took off his shoes like I had been doing it all my life and he seemed to find nothing strange about it.

He stretched again and murmured thanks. He closed his eyes and hummed to the tune that was on the radio. I asked him how old he was and he said eighteen and went back to humming.

We stopped talking and in a few minutes, he was asleep. I just sat there watching him. I still had made no reference to sex at all and here I was sitting there doing nothing about it. I had a beautiful boy in my room and nothing was happening. For me this was unbelievable. I reached over and began to unbutton his shirt. Believe it or not, I still had no thoughts of making him! I lifted him up carefully and removed his shirt. He wore no skivvy shirt. He didn't wake up. He must really be tired. It took me ten minutes to get up enough nerve to remove his slacks. I didn't want him to get them all wrinkled, but I was afraid that if I took those off too, he would awaken and get the wrong idea.

For some reason, I didn't want this boy to dislike me. Finally, I reached over and undid his belt and unzipped his pants. I was so nervous I was shaking like a leaf, and I was suddenly very stimulated. I pulled off his pants and hung them over the chair. Now he lay there in just his shorts. His body was tanned and firm. His skin looked so smooth and unblemished that I couldn't help running my hand over his stomach. Still he didn't stir. I forced myself to stay above the line where his shorts met his stomach. He was completely relaxed and peaceful. I couldn't take my eyes from his face, he looked so serene and childlike in his sleep.

I couldn't help myself, and I leaned over and kissed him. I didn't care if he woke up or not, or if he left right then, I had to kiss him at least once. He stirred slightly, but didn't awaken. I threw caution to the winds and kissed him again, running my hand through his hair. It was very soft and yet he had no oil or grease on it. By this time, I was completely excited and having gone this far, I reached down and ran my hand over the front of his shorts. It was still soft, but as I massaged it, it began to get hard. I moved down and slowly pulled the edge of his shorts until it reached to his ankles.

His meat was beautifully proportioned to the rest of his body. I leaned over and kissed the head and then just watched as it slowly rose and got completely hard. He must be awake now, but I looked up and his eyes were still closed. After going this far, I took the head in my mouth and felt the smoothness of it. I ran my tongue over it and then slowly went down all the way. I felt his body twitch slightly. I refused to look up at him. I didn't want to know if he were awake or not. I started sucking and running my tongue over the underside. I could see his stomach muscles contract and relax as I went up and down on him. I listened for his breathing, but all I could hear was my own. He was evidently determined not to show that he knew what was going on. Maybe he didn't.

I had never been through anything like this in my life. I was sure no one could sleep through a blow job, and yet he showed no response outside of an occasional contraction of muscles. I began working faster and I could feel his meat getting very hot. It was throbbing in my mouth and I knew he was getting close to climax. I went down as far as possible and the head entered my throat. I stayed there for a moment and then slowly came up and then down quickly again. Suddenly he arched his body and I felt his hands on my head forcing me all the way down. This reaction upset me so much that I came at the same time he did. His body twitched again and again as he shot into me and the front of my pants were getting all messed up. Then he was finished and his body relaxed again. I got up, washed his meat with a cloth and pulled up his shorts again. All this time, I still hadn't looked at his face. Now I looked up at him and he was wide awake. I searched his face for some sign of revulsion. There was none. I swallowed and tried to relax. "I'm sorry," I said, "I couldn't help it."

"You don't have to be sorry. I could have stopped you, but I had always heard of this kind of thing, and I wanted to try it out. When I met you today, I wasn't sure if you were one of them or not. But I was so tired and you were friendly so I figured, what the hell."

"Are you sorry you came up?"

"No."

"Good. It doesn't have to ever happen again if you don't want it to."

"I'm not sure whether I do or not. It was different than anything I have ever done before, but it wasn't unpleasant."

So we talked about it and the more I talked to him, the more I had to force myself not to fall in love with him. Eventually, the conversation slowed again and I could see he was very tired. "Lay back and get some sleep, if you like," I said. "I'll leave you alone this time."

"I think I will; I'm so tired. And I'm not worried about you leaving me alone. As I said, it wasn't bad." He smiled and closed his eyes and I felt my stomach flip. I laid down beside him and laid my arm across his stomach. I kissed him once more before he went to sleep and then I too drifted off.

When I woke up he was gone. I told myself I should have expected it, but it still upset me. I wanted him back so bad I hurt. I sent down to room service for coffee and just stayed in my room for the rest of the day. I told myself I should go out cruising to forget it, but I couldn't face up to it. I tried to read and then I tried to watch television, but all I could think of was Alan. Finally about ten o'clock, I decided I had to get out of the room or go buggy. I changed clothes and was just going out the door when I saw him coming up the corridor. I tried to relax but it was no good. Then he was at the door and asked if he could come in. Silly question. We talked and he said that he had been all mixed up and that he had wanted to think it over. Then he had come back. We lay on the bed and talked until very late. Then we got undressed and got into it.

Lying there in the dark with the radio playing very softly and feeling his warm body next to mine drove me out of my mind. I could not keep my hands off of him. But he didn't seem to mind. He said he had decided that this was the way things should be. He wanted to learn all about sex with men. He had a very willing teacher. He spent the whole weekend. That night, after we had lain there talking about it, we decided to go sixty-nine. We got into position and he learned very fast. I told him to take only a little bit at a time and it wasn't long before he was all the way down on me. I told him and showed him how to use his tongue, and he was soon sucking me for all he was worth.

We were both reaching climax too fast, so I told him to stop for a while and I started to play with his ass with my tongue. I kissed it all over and then worked my tongue up into him. It drove him wild and he started to do the same thing to me. You would be surprised how long you can do this without reaching the boiling point. It is the most frustrating thing in the world. I could feel his tongue on and in my ass, and it was just enough to excite me, but not enough to the point of coming. Then I went down on him again and he did the same. By this time we were both very hot and we had both only gone down twice before we came. He locked his legs around my head and shoved in as far as possible. I could feel his body tense, and he made little whimpering sounds as he begged me to come also.

The next morning, I woke up before he did and I raised up on my elbow and just looked at him. My god, he was good-looking! Finally he stirred and opened his eyes. He reached up and pulled me down and kissed me. We lay there for a while not saying anything. I was caressing him and running my hands through his hair and before long, we were both getting excited again. I had planned on going sixty-nine again, but without realizing it, I ended up sitting on his stomach. I could feel his hard cock poling me in the back and so I raised up and gently let it enter my ass. We took it very slow and soon it was all the way in. I began to work it around a little bit and he looked up at me and smiled. "Oh, Ray, it feels so good. Make it last and last and last. I don't want to ever stop."

But of course it would, because we could only hold off so long. He reached up and started to jack me off, and all the time he was raising and lowering his body and writhing around on the bed. He started to moan softly and I knew he was ready. I could feel every inch of his meat inside of me as he fucked wildly. He was jacking me off like mad and I could feel myself ready to come. My body tensed and I threw back my head and whispered his name over and over. "Oh, Alan, Alan, Alan, oh, baby, keep it up, I'm coming."

Then I shot all over his stomach and right after, I felt him freeze as he forced his way up as far as possible. He shuddered and closed his eyes. I watched his face as it changed from passion to ecstasy to relaxation. He held his breath as he came, and his whole body was motionless. Then it was over and we both lay back completely exhausted. We fell asleep again and after waking, I ordered breakfast. Later, I took him back to the base and he promised to come back next weekend. He did. That was two years ago. Now he lives with me and I don't bother cruising any more.

CHAPTER TWO
TWO BOYS AND A TEACHER

Miss Joyce Graham adjusted her heavy horn-rimmed glasses, looked as sternly as possible at the two boys as she could, and said, "Jack and Ernie, you both are to stand in the cloak room until after school when I shall have a serious talk with you." Her patience was at the breaking point, as the big fellows shuffled noisily toward the back of the classroom, punching playfully at each other.

Miss Graham was the new teacher, and how she wished she were anywhere else but way out in this little country schoolhouse with twenty-seven pupils of all grades. *It wouldn't be too bad if it weren't for those two older boys,* she thought to herself. *They should be in high school. They're intelligent enough, but they've missed so much school with farming, that they're dreadfully behind.*

She determined to get them transferred next term, or simply flunk them out for good. They were such a bad influence on the younger boys. Ernie wouldn't have been so bad without Jack, or Jack without Ernie, but their constant jokes played on each other made order practically impossible to maintain. They had even taken lately to mocking her tone of voice—an awful, schoolteachery voice, which she hadn't realized she used until they had made her conscious of it.

At first she'd had them sit at the back of the room, but they couldn't be trusted to themselves, so now she had them in the two seats directly in front of her desk, where, if she had to go the back of the room, she had to step over Ernie's great, long legs; and when she reprimanded him for his sprawling posture, he sat at such a ridiculously straight posture for half a day that the other students tittered every time they caught sight of him. Jack was just as bad; sneaky with his perfectly aimed spit-balls and his guileless look when they hit their mark. Not her, as yet, but she fully expected it.

These boys need companions their own age to teach them the seriousness of education; they need further interests and instruction that I can give them. I'll change my tack with them, she thought. *I'll appeal to them to set an example to the younger ones.* And she allowed herself to dream of a few months ahead, having them help the fourth graders do their sums. *I'll start tonight.*

She pictured the lovely black and orange decorations she had hidden in her desk drawer. When the children came to class next Monday morning, the room would be bright with Halloween streamers, and she would have Jack and Ernie help her with them. Maybe that would start them feeling important and grow-up.

Soon it was time for her pupils to get their wraps and file out; Miss G. started back to the empty cloak-room. Where were they? Had they skipped away from school? She dreaded having to discipline them. Why Ernie was inches taller than she, and Jack almost as tall. She stood there a moment in the wonderful quiet now that the last of the children had bundled up and gone. In the dim light she heard a muffled voice very close and her eye was caught by a glint of light from a hole in the huge rough wooden wall where a knot had become dislodged, directly at eye-level.

Immediately she focused to see what was on the other side. It was the boy's toilet she found herself looking into, and the voices she'd heard were those of Ernie and Jack; they stood in full sight, standing sideways in her line of vision; they were relieving themselves into the trough for that purpose. Miss G's eyes popped at what she saw. Their white penises (she'd never seen one before) dangled out of their open flies, and they were so much bigger than the chaste, classic statues through which she was acquainted with the male form. Ernie, who wore old, faded overalls which he'd almost outgrown, stood closest to her, his big hands slung loosely on his thrust-forward hips, letting a long golden stream flow lazily from the pink head of his thick, long shaft. Jack held his only slightly smaller one nonchalantly in his left hand, and seemed to be guiding it back and forth as though he were wetting a figure eight in the trough.

Miss G. was glad they hadn't gone; she was just about to return to her desk and wait for them to appear when Jack started to talk, and though it made her feel guilty, she decided to listen anyway to what the boys were talking about. Always whispering to each other and nudging. Sometimes she had the feeling they were openly eyeing her. They are just little boys, she almost said to herself. Ernie is fifteen, and Jack, though smaller, sixteen. They were snickering together.

Jack was saying, "She's not so old. I'd fuck her if I got the chance and so would you." He shook the dangling thing in his hand dry, and it began to change from its limp, heavy look, to a springy, straight-out-in-front tautness. Its soft whiteness took on a blush, and its head seemed to point upward, the length and thickness growing, expanding all at once. "She's got big boobies, even if she does dress so as not to show them. I can tell. But the way she does her hair in a knot. And those awful glasses." Miss G's fingers stole to her breasts in the stiffly starched, pleated shirtwaist. She blushed a deep red when she realized it was she they were talking about; watching the two boys standing there looking admiringly at each other's semi-erect penises, she felt a strange flow of excitement course through her, focusing itself between her legs where before she had felt stirring feelings of wanting something badly, more than her finger which from time to time she had desperately introduced.

"She's a cold fish," Ernie said.

"Well, I'm telling you, I bet she'd lay," Jack retorted. "I'd sure give it to her." His big, thick penis, longer and thicker than

Jack's, was rising up, though he hadn't touched it.

"You damn well know we couldn't get Miss G. in a hundred years. But Jesus, Jack, you got me so hot talking about it."

"You better drop your pants, Ernie." The big thing he brandished in his hand now was fully aroused, and stood out from his body in an upward arch, the swollen head of it deep-pink, and throbbing. Ernie was saying, "Okay, if you'll let me do it to you."

Miss G. watched fascinated as Ernie's overalls slipped down his legs; she saw how the roots of his hard member were fringed about with a halo of crisp, brown hair and decorated with a neat round sack which hung tightly beneath. Jack, grabbing him by the hips, wedged the bigger fellow between himself and the trough so that Ernie's round, impudent buttocks faced the smaller boy's impatient tool.

He spit a handful, part of which he spread on his inflamed penis and the rest he introduced between the firm buttocks of squirming Ernie. "Take it easy, Jack," Ernie said. Jack laughed, "You know how bad I want it if I let you fuck me in return. I was sore last Wednesday, after you got me down in the barn." With practiced hands he inserted the inflamed head of his glistening shaft into the ass of the other boy.

"You'll get your turn to fuck my ass." Miss G's eyes bugged out in horror and fascination. Jack bore down with great relish, and in spite of Ernie's moans of discomfort, stabbed his hips forward again and again until he shoved a good four inches of it out of sight. At the same time his arms went around Ernie in a tight embrace and his eyes closed. His breath grew short as he held on and felt the hot, wet constricture of the tightness around his passion-swollen tool.

Miss G. could stand no more. All the unacknowledged frustration fell from her as her fingers dug madly at her clitoris under her dress. She acted quickly; coming out of the half-swoon her senses had allowed her to sink into at the overwhelming sight she had just seen, she determined to stop what was going on, because she wanted the boys so badly herself. She rushed to the door of the boy's toilet and knocked fiercely at it. "Jack and Ernie. I hear you in there. Come out this minute. I want to talk to you."

From their sense of guilt, the boys were very prompt in emerging; so prompt that Jack had buttoned his corduroys wrong. Both boys wore sheepish looks, and she saw that there had not been quite enough time for their erections to go down, judging from the bulges in their flies.

"I know it's not much fun for you boys, not having companions your own age at school," she said, barely composing the violent trembling she felt inside, "but that's no reason to act like babies when you are almost men. I'll be back in a minute." She went into the girl's toilet, determined to become a woman—an attractive woman—and in a few minutes brought quite a transformation to herself. Out came the hair pins and with a few deft strokes of her comb, she brought her red-brown locks into the long bob she had thought too young looking for school. She undid the starched blouse, took it off, and pulled a soft sweater on. She looked squintingly into the mirror through her glasses, then removed them, remembering they were only good for seeing distant objects. Now she looked even younger than her twenty-three years. The drive and excitement that swept her along turned her from a souring old maid into a young, female animal, as intent on stalking its prey as were the young beasts she'd just interrupted in their substitution for what she planned to give them.

When she reentered her room, she went to the desk and half leaned, half sat on the front edge of it, between Jack and Ernie, who sat in their seats directly in front of her. Ignoring Ernie's flush and the nudge that Jack gave him, ignoring their young mouths open in awe and the nudge that Jack gave him, ignoring their admiration at the difference in her appearance, their frank appraisal of the curves of her freed breasts she said, "I want you boys to take an interest, a responsibility in school. So tonight you can start helping me do something to surprise the younger children." She reached around and brought out the orange and black Halloween decorations. "Ernie, there's a ladder in the cloak room. Will you bring it? And Jack, you can sort these cut-out pumpkins and cats and witches. They are to go on the windows."

Jack's mouth didn't close; his eyes were glued on her as she led him to the panes of glass at the north side of the room. "Now see, mix them up; first a cat, then a pumpkin, and so on, with a dab of paste. Get a chair and I'll show you." She did one window while the boys watched, not saying a word. She was absolutely beside herself, watching the wanton passion in their faces, feeling so wanton herself that she purposely caught her dress on the back of the chair and they got a good long glimpse of her shapely legs up past her stockings.

Then Jack, the bulge at his fly angling recklessly up, climbed up and attached a witch to one of the panes of the window.

"Look," she said, "A little more to the center." And she reached up on tiptoe, falling back directly against the boy's groin. Her breasts pushed against him in the spot that she had seen naked and excited only a few minutes before, and she recovered her balance. Now she could see it outlined, thrusting hard against the barrier of corduroy that held it in. She felt a blush rise, and out of the corner of her eye she saw that Ernie had taken in the encounter. She knew that they were both conscious of her blush, but she felt reckless; she wanted them so badly—had to have them, she didn't care how.

Next she was on the ladder with a streamer, trying to tie it to the light fixture while Ernie stood watching. "Steady the ladder, Ernie," she said, and he moved closer. She deliberately nudged against him slightly, and the soft line of her thigh under her smooth skirt pressed against his face. He blushed, but immediately got the idea, and when she moved back his face thrust forward against her, loving the sweet smell and the firmness of her. With one hand he held the ladder, and he grasped the other lightly about a rung, so that the tips of his fingers contacted the inside of her legs, just above the knee. Soon the pressure against her legs became stronger and Ernie's big fingers were quite frankly, though tremulously, caressing her. But now the streamer was tied, and she climbed down. Ernie's face was aglow; his big brown eyes avoided hers. He fidgeted nervously with the streamers, aware that something wonderful was up, but not quite believing it. The strain of his erection on those old denim overalls was terrific.

Miss G's eyes took it in hungrily as she felt for the first time a surrender to the flesh. She noticed that Jack was hanging pumpkins and cats sidewise and upside down in his eagerness to watch what was going on between her and Ernie.

"Oh no," she said, and rejoined Jack. "Hang them straight, Jack," and this time she made no pretense but stood with her sweater-clad breasts an inch from Jack's fly. Slowly he pressed it forward until she felt that hard gristle of his inflamed penis against her firm, virgin mounds. "You mean like that?" he asked, and he pushed his cocky manhood against her. She realized the insinuation in the boy's remark, and it frightened her. For several moments she allowed herself the delight of the super-drugged contact, and then realized that if she allowed herself to be had by these boys, they might not keep quiet about it. She drew away quickly, "Yes, that's it."

As yet she'd actually done nothing, and if she controlled herself, perhaps she could forget the whole thing. So she returned warily to Ernie who, on the rickety ladder, was tying the rest of the center streamers. She held the ladder straight, trying to keep her distance, but the dazzle, the delicious temptations, were too much for her.

When the boy edged one of his big legs forward, and she felt the soft, worn denim smelling so clean and masculine, she lost all sense and let him push his thigh against her face. Ernie, seeing that she allowed the familiarity, pressed harder, moving down a step; and then she felt the hard, round end of his magnificent erection digging into her temple. For a few seconds she clung there, her heart pounding, her whole being given up to passion, and then, feeling the boy boldly rub that hard knob of manhood in its thin denim into her face, the shock, the too-sudden release of all her pent-up months and years was too much for her; she fainted dead away at the foot of the ladder.

The boys came instantly to her and pulled her gently up and laid her down on a long bench. Ernie said, "What'll we do? Get some water? Get the doctor?" But Jack was way ahead of him. "Can't you see that she's hot for us? Didn't she let you rub your cock against her like she did me? Gee, now that she's out cold, let's have some fun with her."

So they pulled the blinds as a precaution against someone discovering them, and they soon had Miss G's clothes pulled up from her very intimate parts. Ernie fell excitedly to her lovely breasts, pulling her sweater up above them, and began kissing them and getting such a charge out of the sensation of their firm softness that he unconsciously unbuttoned his overalls and started to fondle his big rod.

Jack was more interested in her soft, flat belly and creamy thighs. He soon had her panties pulled way down one white leg, and discovered the cleft between her shapely legs that started out with a tuft of downy, auburn hair and soon developed into a pair of velvety pink lips which his trembling fingers explored, gently prodding her inflamed clitoris, sticking one finger into the opening until he was too hot and had to let his pants drop to free his burning cock.

Both boys were thus employed, gently exploring and fondling, breathlessly kissing her, when Miss G. gradually came back to consciousness. For a moment she felt sure this was a strange erotic dream, but she soon realized that the wonderful pressures, and hot kisses she felt, the sighs and moans she heard, the hot fingers pressing, the hot lips sucking the very part of her that cried out to be touched and kissed, was all deliciously real.

She opened her eyes to a mere slit and saw that both boys were bent ever her, pulling on their fully erect penises, touching and kissing her all over gently in order not to waken her, afraid to try anything further.

Jack stood with his sturdy legs wedged between hers; she felt them squirm. Felt the throbbing of his whole body as the movement of his hot masturbation emanated from his trembling thighs. Almost involuntarily, she started to moan in sheer pleasure. Both boys started at the sound, and as she opened her eyes she saw them trying quickly to get themselves covered. They were panic-stricken. Ernie started to run to the door, Jack following him.

"Jack, Ernie," her voice was a hoarse whisper, "come here this minute," and they wheeled almost reluctantly and returned to her side, their faces white. Without moving, she said, "You're not going to leave me like this, are you? Nothing like this has ever happened to me before, but now that you've started, you've just got to finish. And if either one of you ever dare to tell...." Their mouths hung open as they realized what she meant, and they felt as sick inside as she did at the prospect.

"Oh God, no," Jack vowed.

"Lock the door, Ernie," she said, and he hurried away to do it. They were both standing awkwardly at her side. "Let's take our clothes off," she said, and the two hot youths and the young woman were soon naked together, all breathless. "Have you boys ever done it?" she panted, and Jack said, "I used to do it to my cousin May before she moved," Ernie said bashfully. "I never had a girl."

"Then," she said, lying down again on the bench, loving the look of their stiff penises jutting out so close, their strong, hairless bodies so smooth, "Jack, you do it first, since you know how. Do what you were doing before, Ernie." And the bigger boy's hungry lips immediately found the rosy nipples of her breast. How she loved the feeling of his ripe lips sucking there, helping to draw all of the hot sex of her to the surface. And how that big Ernie sucked! His hands sought and then he forced one of his arms under her at the waist, pulling her toward him, tentatively at first to caress her. She put one of her arms over the strong curve of his back, drawing his broad, smooth chest closer to her; the other she ran into his thick blond hair, pulling his mouth so hard against her naked breast that she felt his teeth.

Jack set, tremblingly, to work at once, his hard thighs hot

against hers; his fingers gently prodding, teasing her burning vagina, getting its soft lips ready for entry. Now she felt his hands on her lips and then a new pressure, one so soft in texture, yet so infinitely hard, so hot, so demanding! He was introducing the thick broad head of his stone-hard tool into the narrow mouth of her vagina, and the touch of it to that virgin hot spot sent her into ecstasies, so that involuntarily, she tensed her body, sending forward those eager lips the faster to admit the desired object.

"Christ, it's tight, Miss Graham." Now, carefully Jack squirmed it in one tiny nudge after another, his taut sturdy body bent over her lovingly, every fiber trembling. Ernie was watching now, his mouth agape, seeing the big head of Jack's tool disappear at last.

Miss G's mouth was watering from the deliciously painful sensation of it. She was almost dazed, and her lips sought Ernie's smooth shoulder eagerly half-kissing, half-biting. A moment later she felt the firm lips on her soft ones and they both almost went out of their minds at the contact.

Jack had at last touched bottom; his penis was half-in, and so hard, so tightly in that hot velvety hole, that he felt he could neither withdraw nor advance it. So he squirmed, and angled his hips, round and back, gently at first, but then becoming overwhelmed in an ocean of maddening feeling. He managed to back off slightly and thrust forward with all his strength, bracing his strong legs against the bench.

Miss G. was wincing, hurt, not knowing which she felt more, pleasure or pain, but she bore up bravely under the tough little fellow's deep prodding, until she felt an unutterable twinge of pain which made her faint. Her maidenhead had popped, and now to Jack's delight his big member slid with little difficulty all the way in. She lay there unconscious as Jack's little behind rose, and then plunged down in great, satisfying thrusts. The boy was approaching his climax, feeling the wonderful tightness about his distended penis drawing on it, pulling forward as deep as he could thrust, he suddenly felt it start and flow completely spasmodic, thrashing about almost losing his balance, as the hot wonderful sperm shot deep into the girl's body.

The minute the bigger boy saw that his buddy was no longer in action, he was standing tensely at his side, trying to pull him off so he, too, could satisfy himself. Ernie stood awkwardly alongside them, his big hand searching for pockets in his nakedness. He was so close that she could feel the little blond sprouts of hair on his legs tickling her arm. She loved the clean hardness of his young body, loved his sex-hungry mouth, half-open, hardly believing in the heavenly experience.

There was something rather fearsome in the proportions of his most beautiful of all features. Miss G. expected to be hurt; she had heard about that, but her pleasure-racked senses wouldn't allow her to think about anything but their gratification. Her glance turned to the smaller boy. She loved every bit of him. His trembling dark hair, the short breaths he took as gently, patiently, he eased the penetrations. His thick, broad shoulders and big, sturdy legs could have sent his burning-hot rod into her like a battering ram, and she knew it and loved him for his restraint.

Jack held on for dear life; his stiff cock's big load spent, but still hard as a stone, and just primed and ready to start again.

"Christ, let me have her," Ernie pleaded.

"Aw, gee, Ernie, I came so damned fast. Let me just have one more fuck, then it'll be all the easier for you." And he started ramming her again.

"Damn, it gets me so hot watching you fuck her. Look here," said Ernie, "if I can't fuck her, I'll fuck you," and he was too strong, too hot to be put off. Besides, Jack was in such heaven that he'd have gone through any kind of torture to maintain his present position. Ernie had soon lubricated his rod and his little friend's anus, and was forcing the huge thing into the hot tightness. He had some difficulty at first, but soon as the big head had found its place securely between Jack's cheeks, it slipped in fairly easily, inch by inch, and Ernie found that it was hardly necessary to move to have the most wonderful feeling, for

Jack's hot little ass was squirming about and beating forward and back madly, so he just put his arms around Jack and clung there, letting his buddy's hard little cheeks pull and his hot asshole squeeze and squeeze his burning tool.

"Goddamn you, Ernie, I'll get even with you," Jack said when he felt the big boy give a couple of deep jabs into him, but the expression on his face belied his voice. Though Ernie had a tight grasp around Jack's middle, the smaller boy seized his chance to lie flat on top of the girl, pulling Ernie down with him. Jack kissed her breasts and throat and lips, ran his hands through her hair and drove his gleaming rod harder than ever into her. Ernie became more active, driving in on Jack's off beat, so that when Jack's ass was turned up ready for the downward plunge, it got as much of Ernie's rod as it could hold.

Miss G. was beginning to feel again the pain that had made her faint, but diminished this time by deep and growing stimulation that Jack's hot young member was bringing her, blotted out everything else but pleasure.

Jack noticed that she stirred slightly and he nudged Ernie, who understood and reluctantly withdrew immediately; he slipped quickly out to the boys' room and washed his penis and was at Miss G's side by the time she opened her eyes, again kissing her lips and breasts. Jack had given up his position flat on top and was crouched over her, allowing Ernie room to get at her breast. He was full of steam, moaning with sheet ecstasy, getting so hot he started talking under his breath. "Oh, baby is that good—oooh, what a hot little cunt."

Miss G. responded madly, pushing her hips to meet his forward onslaught to the point where she'd have a climax coming soon. "Oh, God, it's wonderful," she whispered.

"Gee, I wish mine was in it," Ernie moaned. He was so beside himself that he started unconsciously to jerk off his tool, inches from the girl's face. She wanted it so badly. Ernie was carried away, his legs bent at the knees and his hand whacking away. No, she wanted to touch it, to feel it against her body. She reached up tentatively and her fingers felt his big testicles, which were firm and moist with his slight perspiration. At her touch Ernie moaned slightly and slackened his speed of jerking off to almost nothing, he was so close to coming.

Jack got hotter than ever when he saw the girl fondling his buddy's big balls so close to his face. Miss G. had her fingers on Ernie's pulsating cock now, and Ernie panted breathlessly to her: "God, I can hardly wait to get it in there. What's it like, Jack?" he asked.

"Oooh, it's so hot and wet and tight!! Jesus, it's good!!!"

Ernie's hand slid back and forth over his big slick thing. "Let me make it hot and wet for you," she said, and pulled the boy's tool to her burning lips. Jack was ready anyway, but the sight of her lips and tongue licking the broad, round, glistening head of that cock made him throw his load in her.

Ernie's big shaft bobbed against her chin and throat as it threw out a great thick stream of creamy white come, splattering down her breast and belly and hitting Jack's shoulders and face. "Oh Christ," he said. "That got it!" Miss G. was climaxing too, sending out deep spurts of her own hot discharge to match those of Jack and Ernie.

The two boys collapsed momentarily on either side of her on the bench. They had never spent such an hour in their lives, and Miss G., lying there hurt and inflamed and torn, was the most exhausted of all. She felt conscience and reason along with pain, flooding back to her; yet she had so shattered her normal pattern that she could not go back to it. She wished that she could vanish into thin air; she lay there forever so long, just not allowing herself to think.

Then she heard Ernie say, "Gosh, Miss G., it's getting dark. Guess we better all run along, huh? If you feel like meeting me, I'll be down by the mill about noon, Sunday," he whispered. She shuddered slightly at the thought of added pain to her sore body. His arm was there to gently help her to her feet and Jack was gathering her scattered clothes and trying to help her dress.

"Now, don't tell a soul, or I won't let you do it again," she said, and the three shadows left the dark school house to go their separate ways.

That night, after falling asleep immediately after she bathed, dinnerless, and having thrown herself into bed, Miss G. woke, and although she was still a little sore, she thought of her two angel boys and relived the afternoon's experience as well as she could. With a smile on her face, she sank back into a deep sleep.

"I told you she was plenty hot," Jack was saying, "and you said we'd never fuck her in a hundred years."

"What do you mean, 'we?' I still haven't fucked her, but I'm sure as hell fucking you!"

Jack had no sooner put out his light that night when his buddy tapped on the window, and after being let in, stripped off and crawled into bed with him and at first by sheer strength forced him to submit. Now Jack was relaxed, letting Ernie pound that hot column into his little ass. The strong, firm body of the bigger boy pressed hard against him, and he realized, feeling his own erect cock, that he really didn't mind it. "Well," he said, "you got her to suck yours."

"Yeah," responded Ernie, and the thought of it combined with the movement to make the orgasm in him well up and shoot.

After Ernie had shot, he crept out the window, leaving Jack to come as best he could. Jack lay awake thinking, instead of pulling his dick. He could hardly believe what had happened with the new teacher; it puzzled him that such a "lady" would be so passionate. Lots of things puzzled Jack—his feeling for Ernie. He liked to be with him for one thing because he was so big and good-looking. He liked to talk Ernie into a hard-on and watch it bulge out the front of his overalls, but it was something more, too! Jack wasn't entirely innocent, of course. That fooling around with his brother Rud, had just been child's play; but last year there had been a traveling salesman. Seemed like a nice enough guy, who hired Jack to run errands, and who had sucked him off eight times in one day. He had been a fairy, you could tell by the way he walked, and Jack hated to think about him because he didn't want to turn into any fairy, and yet, with Miss G. and all the other women to think about, there he was thinking about Ernie fucking him and him fucking Ernie. While he beat the daylights out of his cock, all he could picture was Ernie's cock coming closer, and he knew sucking it was going to make him hotter than anything.

Several times the next day Joyce thought about the boys, and even when she didn't consciously picture them, she felt the awakening they brought her. She was all over the pain. Now the slight irritation she felt was just enough to keep her deliciously conscious of the wonderful pleasures of sex. In a way she dreaded school on Monday, having to be so close to them, and wanting them. She wondered how it could all end.

Ernie worked very hard on Saturday so that he could be sure and have Sunday afternoon to meet the pretty teacher at the mill. When Jack came by that afternoon, and wanted him to come out to the barn, he put him off, knowing Jack wanted sex. Jack knew something about the Sunday date with Joyce, and he wanted sex so badly that he went home feeling resentful and very horny. His twenty-one-year-old brother, Rudley, was in town, with his truck, to haul a load of produce back to Butte, and Jack found himself wondering eagerly if Rud would like to have sex with him. (It was Rud who had first bent him to his will some years before; but he had married at eighteen and moved to another town. They hadn't had an encounter in over three years.) His brother was about Ernie's build, not such a big penis as his, but very sexy, and at dinner, Jack's eyes sought Rud's so often—finally being rewarded by Rud's sly wink that Rud asked him when the meal was through and they stood on the porch smoking, "What's on your mind, Jack?"

Jack answered soon enough, "COCK!"

His brother laughed and said he'd thought so. Jack, in order to get Rud in the mood, told him about having Joyce (not telling him who she was or anything,) and Rud did seem to get rather hot, but he laughed, and said, "Well great, send her around when she wants a real fuck."

"What are you doing tonight?" Jack asked him.

"I've got a hot old widow lined up," he said, and going inside he grabbed his leather jacket and over his shoulder he said, "see you, Jack," and drove off in the big, empty truck.

* * * * * * *

Sunday about ten o'clock, Ernie worked painfully for an hour over a note to Joyce telling her to please be at the mill by one o'clock—that he would be waiting. He crossed out the word please and reinserted it, gave the note to his seven-year-old brother with instructions to get a yes or no answer—and the death penalty for losing the note on the way.

Jack, hoping to find his brother in bed, and possibly persuading him to give him the hot sex he wanted so badly, was disappointed to find that Rud hadn't come home. So he shuffled down to the town aimlessly, too piqued at Ernie to seek him out.

On his way he saw Ernie's little brother on the road ahead, overtook him, and walked at his side. "I've got a note for the teacher," he boasted. After a slight struggle, Jack had the note in his hand. The little boy's screams and tears finished immediately when Jack gave it back. "I'll go along and help you," Jack said. They were on the main block now and there was Rud's truck parked by the barber shop. On Sunday, as every day, it served as a social gathering place, and Rud was inside talking to three older men. Jack's brain zoomed up with an idea. Grabbing Ernie's brother's hand he went to the barber shop door and told Rud he wanted to talk to him.

"You want the girl I told you about?" Jack asked when they were outside.

"Sure, send her around," Rud laughed.

"I'm not kidding. I think you can have her today." And they walked up the street toward Mrs. Grove's boarding house. "You go deliver the note," he said, and sent the boy the rest of the way alone. "And stop here on your way back." Then he told Rud about the deal at the mill.

Rud at first said, "She'd know I wasn't the guy."

"Honest, you and Ernie are darn near the same build and

the mill is real dark." At some length Jack convinced him to go there a few minutes before one o'clock.

"What do you get out of it?" Rud asked, slyly.

"Well, I'm sore at Ernie," Jack answered, and then thinking ahead, added, "But let's see. You could let me go on your next hunting trip."

"Okay, that's gonna be next weekend, and six of the fellows from my ball team in Butte are going up to the ridge cabin Friday night."

"What did she say?" asked Jack when the fellow was back.

"She said 'yes,'" he repeated. In a few minutes Rud, with Jack's help, had written a note for Ernie's brother to take to him to read. "Yes, I'll be there, but please leave the mill as soon as you get this note, and don't come back until two o'clock. I am so afraid of being followed."

Rud bought the kid a candy bar, and warned him to say the lady had given him the note. They went around to the mill, cautiously looking through the bushes along the stream to make sure Ernie had left and wasn't concealed and watching. Rud went inside and found the bed of blankets that Ernie had made on the floor on an inner room, inky dark. In a few minutes Jack joined him inside the mill and Rud asked more about Joyce. Jack told him about her firm breasts and how hot and tight she was. He described feeling her maidenhead break as he rammed himself into her.

After about five minutes their eyes became accustomed to the dark and they could see each other sitting in the dark on the blankets. Jack began to feel his brother's urgency in his voice. Rud was plenty excited, impatient for sex. "It must be damn near time for her to show up," he whispered.

"Think I'll take all my clothes off and be all ready," Rud answered.

"When I hear her coming I'll slip back of the partition and scram," Jack said; he could hear Rud's jeans whipping off his legs, the sounds of his shirt and jacket being taken off, and those big boots clumped down on the floor. There was enough light to see the outline of his tall brother as he stood above him, and Jack couldn't help but see that his penis was bobbing out at a right angle to his body.

"Remember," Rud whispered, "how I used to fuck you?"

Jack reached up and took Rud's big, hard thing in his hand. "I sure do," he breathed. "I used to hate it at first."

"Yeah, then it got so you'd follow me around to get it and I couldn't leave you alone. Been so damn busy fucking my wife and any other girl I could get hold of, but every once in awhile I *see* your tight little ass and get a hard-on from it." Rud reached down and pulled his brother to his feet. "Take down your jeans a minute, kid," His lips were right at Jack's ear. Rud's big hands were on his chunky little cheeks and then the younger boy felt the dull thud of Rud's erect penis against him. Rud's finger sought for his little hole and in a moment he felt the big head probing there. Just then there was a creaking, rustling noise, and Jack grabbed his jeans back on and noiselessly dashed back of the partition, "Damn," he thought, "I sure wish I'd got that."

"Joyce?" whispered Rud's voice, as Jack had coached him.

There was a moment's pause, then a whispered, "Yes."

"Come on in," he said, and as she came in sight he reached out his hand and took one of hers. "Mmmm," he murmured, and drew her close to his naked body and started his hands roaming over her. "Take off your clothes, baby," he said, and soon Jack could see from his post behind the partition, their two bodies locked together. They were lying down on the blanket, a tangle of naked arms and legs, and he could hear the sucking sounds of lips on breasts, lips on lips.

Though he would have loved to stay and watch, Jack slipped out. He took up a spot in the bushes where he'd see Ernie come across the fields to the mill. He hadn't been waiting long when the big, good-looking boy came striding along. Jack sauntered out of the bushes very casually and met his friend.

"Hi, Ernie," he said brightly.

"What are you snooping around for?" Ernie asked.

"Well," Jack lowered his voice and put his hand on Ernie's

arm to stop him just a few yards from the mill. "Miss G. is in there."

"I know she is," Ernie's voice was an impatient whisper as he strode to the door.

"I don't think you ought to go in," said Jack.

"Why in the hell not? She's expecting me."

"Are you sure?"

"Sure, I made a date to lay her."

"And she's being laid right now."

"I don't believe it."

"Okay, come on in, only be real quiet, and see for yourself."

Jack went on, and they started on tiptoe, toward the door. "She's getting a real fuck by someone who really knows how." Jack led the way, taking Ernie's hand until they were back of the partition, just a few inches from the blanket where Rud and Miss G. lay. It was too dark to see, but there were deep sighs and moans of pleasure and the solid thwack sound repeated again and again of two desiring bodies coming together with terrific tension, heavy breathing, kissing and gurgling noises, soft female murmurs and moans, and all of a sudden a husky male whisper. "You like that nice big cock in there, don't you honey? You really love getting fucked, don't you?"

"Oh yes, God knows I love it. Oh Jesus, it's wonderful. That's twice you've made me come. Oh, God, keep giving it to me, Ernie, I'm almost there again."

"Don't worry baby, you'll get it all. I'm not half through yet."

It was light enough now to make out their bodies and Ernie watched Rud's white ass rise and fall in a steady, pounding movement, saw Miss G's body quivering under each thrust. Jack and Ernie jammed their bodies tight together till they could both see all that happened through the break in the partition. Ernie, straining the big protruding curve of his erection (still sheathed in his overalls) against his little friend's leg.

The sight of the girl he'd expected to meet being cocked so ably was so frustrating, yet exciting, that it made him doubly hot. He wanted to tear in and pull the other fellow off and have her himself, and yet it was so wonderful to watch and listen to that happen, and he was furious with him, yet he was so hot that slowly, automatically, he unbuttoned his fly and let his taut organ spring free.

Jack was stripping his out too, and when he felt his buddy's big throbbing rod shove against his legs, he let his jeans fall so that Ernie's too, touched the smooth bare flesh of his thigh. Then he inched his way about so that his firm buttocks bore the brunt of the hot pressure that his big friend exerted.

Rud kept up his rhythmic strokes, getting the girl so hot that she kept whispering things to him, things which made Ernie's passion soar higher so that his hand finally grasped his cock and started to flog it unmercifully. Jack whispered to the boy, "You can fuck my ass, if you want, Ernie," but Ernie paid no attention to him, just went on beating himself off as he watched and listened to the hot couple.

In desperation, Jack tried to grab the other's cock and worm his tight little ass right around it...but Ernie brushed him away and would not let go...all the while pounding on that throbbing dick of his. Miss G. and Rud mounted into a frenzy of sighing and moaning.

Rud was just about to slam his second big load of come into her, to pack her brimful, and Jack, carried away by the sight and sound, and wanting Ernie so badly, decided that since his buddy refused to fuck him, he was bound to have his big cock one way or another. All of a sudden he remembered his dream of sucking it. Remembering how Ernie seemed to enjoy having Joyce do it, he gradually slid to his knees between Ernie's legs and put out his lips to the big head of Ernie's dong. Half hypnotized, Ernie kept on beating off his cock, his fist at the end of each stroke hitting Jack full in the mouth. As soon as the big fellow began to react to the delicious feeling of being sucked, he stopped his violent jerking while thrill after thrill pulsated through his body. He stabbed his meat frantically into Jack's throat again and again, holding the smaller boy's head tight in both hands until Jack could scarcely keep from gagging.

Rud was all ready now, and Joyce was in heaven, feeling her body respond a third time as his wild onslaught continued. He was plowing her now, making each hot thrust of his powerful back as long and deep as he could, as he quickly and surely approached his orgasm. Though Jack's cock only scraped against Ernie's rough boot when he felt the big column in his mouth throb spasmodically and Ernie's whole body shuddered, he couldn't hold back, and as Ernie shot deep into his throat and filled his mouth with the spicy taste, his own rod popped a big thick load on Ernie's boots. A moment later, the lovers on the blanket were also at the end of their mad gyrations and lay there panting.

In a matter of seconds, Rud snatched his clothes on and left while Miss G. lay as though stunned. Jack nudged Ernie and whispered, "Now is your chance." And Ernie, who didn't need a second invitation, at once crept out onto the blanket at the girl. After removing his clothes, he bent over her, and in her ear asked; "Ready for another one?" For though he'd just shot a huge, hot load into Jack's mouth, the touch of her body made his cock as rigid as steel.

"Oh no; help me up, and let's get dressed and get out of here. I must get back. Another time, Ernie."

So she left the mill, going on alone through the tiny village. When she was out of earshot, Jack couldn't help it, he roared with laughter. Ernie turned on him and tried to catch him. He was so furious at that moment, he was sputtering. He could have killed him if he could have caught him, but Jack was quick, and when they reached the door, Ernie realized he was still naked. Then he laughed too, went back in and dressed and the two of them sat on the grass bank laughing over the story, as Jack, tears streaming down his cheeks, told it. It was a good joke on her, too. Suddenly Ernie became grave.

"Look, no kidding, no more tricks, see Jack? I've gotta fuck that girl, see, and you gotta help me instead of getting every-body else there before me."

At school she and the boys avoided each other's eyes by mutual consent. They were quiet and attentive, completely changed from unruly boys to model students. Wednesday afternoon was hot, and school seemed long and tedious. In the middle of the geography lesson, Miss G. let her eyes glance toward Jack. Her eyes were practically undressing him, seeing his round, hard shoulders, and his trim trunk thickly muscled under his faded shirt. She caught sight of his jeans, and saw that he had a large erection. A quick glance at his face revealed the hunger there. She didn't happen to see that he was staring at Ernie. Ernie was even worse. He had one hand in his overall pocket gently massaging himself, and his eyes, which caught hers for a second, were full of hot longing. He blushed a deep pink at her look.

At about 3:30 she stood in the aisle, between the two boys' desks, and asked if they'd stay and help her correct papers.

When the others had left, Miss G. trembled in excitement, and the two boys seemed rooted in their seats, hot with desire. She called them to her desk where they stood one on either side of her, trembling in anticipation. Impulsively, she unfastened their two flies, and put their hard, glistening cocks, unsheathed, in her two hands. She was about to have Ernie pull the blinds and lock the door when there was a sound. It was old Gabe, the man who came now and then to wash the windows and clean the floors. What a narrow escape; the boys corrected test papers for an hour, looking very crestfallen, and though she'd liked to have met them later somewhere, she realized she must be more careful, so she went home, dying to be relieved of the hot desire she felt.

That night, Jack again tried to get Ernie to fuck him, but he said he just couldn't have sex again until he'd got into Miss G. Jack suggested they take her to the cabin for the weekend, and borrow his dad's pick-up truck; not mentioning that Rud and his pals from the ball team were also going.

Next day, Ernie approached her during lunch hour and asked her if she'd go along Friday evening after school. Miss

G. accepted at once, for she had to have some more of this wonderful sex, and an out-of-the-way place like the cabin seemed to her an ideally safe place to let the two boys fuck her all weekend. She told the landlady a cousin was driving up from Butte to take her away for the weekend.

* * * * * * *

So as not to arouse suspicion, they picked her up at a fork in the road behind the school. She had brought hiking clothes, and changed into them. In the back of the truck were blankets and all their provisions, etc. Jack suggested that Miss G. and Ernie ride in back so that no one would see her. So Ernie boosted her up and handed the large bags of food she had cooked especially for the occasion. They wrapped up in the blankets and immediately fell to kissing and feeling each other. However, Jack knew that they couldn't really have sex, because of the bumpy roads ahead.

Unconsciously, he was doing everything possible to keep Ernie from fucking her, in order to have him, himself. He pictured Ernie's big penis, and as he sped along the mountain road, he got very excited. At a point where he knew there'd be no more houses to pass, he stopped and told the two to get out from the back into the cab. Miss G. sat in the middle, and soon she held a hot cock in each hand.

Ernie was so hot he wanted to spread blankets on the ground and have her right then, but Jack said they must hurry to get all settled before dark. There was a half-mile when they reached the end of the road.

On reaching the cabin they set to work getting in wood and soon had a roaring fire going, both in the cookstove at one side of the room, and in the fireplace on the other. They lighted kerosene lamps and Joyce put a big casserole dish in the oven to warm while Ernie and Jack spread blankets on the big double bed. Jack went to a spring nearby to get water and when he got back, Ernie and Joyce were in a hot embrace on the bed. It looked as though they were going to do it right then, but the dinner was ready so they sat and ate it, very hungry after the hike. While Joyce did the dishes the boys lay on the bed before the crackling fire. Jack slowly stripped off and removed Ernie's big boots and then his overalls while he lay pretending to be exhausted. He'd done it before. He just couldn't see or feel enough of that boy's big handsome body and that beautiful cock.

It wasn't long before they'd pulled her down between them and stripped her of her clothes. She felt a hot body on each side of her, lips kissing and sucking her all over. Somehow Jack jockeyed himself into the more advantageous position and soon he was spreading her legs, to Ernie's frustration, getting ready to sink his hot rod in her. The bigger boy was just about to yank him away from her when Jack managed to squeeze the head of his dick between the soft tight lips of her vulva, and Joyce threw her arms about Jack's back, holding him close, while he pushed the rest of it deeper and deeper. "Jesus, you're a bastard Jack," Ernie exploded. "It's not enough that you get your brother to lay her while she thinks I'm doing it. Now when I really get my first chance, you slip in ahead again. I'll go nuts if I don't get in there."

"Your brother?" Joyce asked. "In the mill?"

"Uh huh," he answered. "I was gonna tell you. He thought you were terrific."

"Gosh, it was wonderful. And here I thought it was Ernie. You're certainly full of surprises, but I must say I didn't mind that one. I'm sorry, though, Ernie. Jack, why don't you let Ernie have me first? You can have me right after. I just can't get enough."

"I'm afraid that isn't the last surprise," Jack said, nervously as he crawled off. There were voices outside. "You'll get plenty of fucking tonight."

Miss G. reached for something to cover herself as the door opened and Rud came in followed by his six teammates, all tall young fellows. But the second Jack had let go, Ernie came in close to her, forcing her back on the bed, angling his big erect cock into position, completely ignoring their arrival.

"Well, what do you know, a party!" Rud said. "Jack, introduce us to the lady. I'm Rud, Jack's brother," he went on, not giving Jack a chance to speak.

"I've heard about you," Miss G. said tartly. "Oh Ernie, please stop pawing me," and she sat up, pushing him off while his poor frustrated cock throbbed. "You may call me Joyce. I wasn't prepared for such a big crowd. Why don't you put on a big pot of coffee, Jack?" she went on. "In fact, I didn't expect anyone except Jack and Ernie."

"Well, you get a treat, cause you can have all of us."

The fellows were all lined up, staring at her. Rud introduced them. "This is Vic," he said, indicating a tall stocky Italian boy about twenty; "and Swede, he's a sports writer on the Butte Eagle. The rest of these guys are on my ball team." Swede smiled.

He was a very good looking lad, twenty-three, tall, blond, well built. "Meet Frank," Rud went on, pushing forward a tall lanky blond American boy, just over average height, nineteen. "Flash," twenty-one, big, stocky, graceful, black-eyed. "And Brick," who was lanky with almost black-reddish hair, twenty years old. All of them were nice-looking and athletically built. All of them dressed in western clothes, Rud wearing jeans, denim jacket, driver's cap and heavy leather lumber-jack boots. Vic with skin-tight khaki frontier pants, and western suede jacket and high jack-boots. Swede wearing a short suede jacket, army pants and heavy motorcycle boots. Frank and Brick were dressed alike with motorcycle leather jackets, army pants, and heavy motorcycle boots. Lon dressed like Rud, except for his tight jeans stuck inside his lumber-jack boots that came high up to his knees.

Jack had pulled on his jeans, and served coffee all around, and Rud asked Miss G. if she wanted them to stay or go. After a few minutes consideration, she decided it would be wonderful to have them all and said she wanted them to stay if they'd go easy on her because she was new at it. They were all getting very horny and Rud suggested they draw lots, after asking Miss G. who she wanted first. Ernie, whose erection hadn't gone down through it all, spoke up and told them he deserved it first. He told how Jack had kept him from having her. "That brother of yours is a little bastard. Why, he even sucked me off to keep me from getting it."

Rud looked at Jack, and the boy blushed. "Oh, you sucked him off, huh? Well, maybe you can keep the boys busy while they're waiting their turn." He reached over and grasped Jack's arm and pulled him over to him. Ernie at once mounted Miss G. and started to insert his tantalized cock.

Rud jerked his fly open and let his jeans fall about his ankles. "You can start with me, Jack," and he shoved his big, thick-headed cock, almost as big as Ernie's, into the boy's face. Jack shrank away. He wanted Rud's cock, wanted it badly, but in front of all these others he just couldn't. "Help me, you guys," Rud said, and Frank and Vic came over and held the boy, who struggled violently a few moments, until Rud forced the huge cock between his lips. Jack's forehead lay against the soft hair of Rud's hard belly, as the big tool pumped in and out of his hot mouth. Miss G. could see it all, and it made her so damned hot, watching Rud's animal lust as he literally fucked the boy's face. Ernie was giving her a wonderful lay; he was just about to come, body stiffening.

Flash was watching the hot sex, bending over, one hand fondling Joyce's breast, and Brick was right next to him, so impatient that he was fingering his cock through his pocket. Joyce loved it; she wished she could take them all at once. She reached up and put her hand against Flash's cock and he unbuttoned his jeans and popped it out into her fingers. It was a big one, nearly as long as Ernie's. Lustily, Joyce squeezed and stroked its long foreskin, pulling it back to expose the thick, round head.

"Come on kid, fuck her," Flash breathed. Brick quickly undid his jeans too, and she had one in each hand. Brick's was so big around she could just circle it with her hand, short and stubby but very thick. He pulled back, saying, "Oh, you better not, or I'll come." Joyce just then started to come, and Ernie, too. "I'm getting my rocks," he whispered, and she felt the hot liquid flooding into her. At the same time Jack felt Rud's ass beginning to contract and he knew he'd be getting his brother's big load.

"What action; what a cocksucker," Rud panted. Jack was in heaven, in spite of the fact that the big fellow was rough with him, jamming his meat full force as deep as he could, Jack's tongue played over and under the slick hard thing and his teeth gave little short resistances that made Rud want to plunge it in all the faster. Lon and Vic and Frank had turned to watch Joyce and Ernie on the bed; only Swede was next to them, silently watching the youth suck hungrily now, his hands on his brother's ass. Kneeling at Rud's feet, Jack was so carried away that his own cock seemed almost to come in his jeans.

"Oh Christ, that got it," moaned Rud, and his hard rod started to spurt its big white, globs of gism into the boy's throat.

Rud had to step in a moment later to defend Ernie's right to stay on and have Joyce again if he felt like a second right away. He pushed Flash, who was making all the racket, around to where Jack, still breathless, still knelt on the floor. "Try that; it's sensational," Rud persuaded him, and Flash, hot as hell anyway, lost no time in getting his tool into the boy's mouth.

Jack felt that he had to put up some kind of a struggle and he tried to avoid Flash's cock, but the guy was too quick. At first Jack didn't like it. He tried to resist, but Flash grabbed his head and held it tight, and gradually the lad cooperated. He then got so hot he unbuttoned Flash's top trouser button and unloosened his belt so that his jeans slid down. There was a rich, masculine, almost animal scent to him that excited Jack. The boy then played with Flash's big balls, ran his fingers over his hard cheeks; Flash flexed and flexed and drove his hot weapon deep until with a gasp, he let go a tremendous flood of gamey-tasting hot sperm. "Wow," he said.

Swede was close by, taking it all in, his pants bulging, and

Flash asked him, "You gonna try it next?"

Swede smiled and said, "Naw, I think I'll wait." Jack tried to catch Swede's eyes; he wanted him above all the others, but the tall blond seemed deliberately to avoid his glance.

Vic was the next one to approach Jack. He had completely removed all his clothes, keeping on only his boots, revealing a neatly patterned body with hairy chest and legs that the boy liked very much. His cock bobbed before him, just the tip of its big head showing. As he stood there a moment before inserting it, Jack smelled a heavy, sweetish odor that he recognized as the smell of a foreskin. For a second it repelled him, but then all of a sudden he found it exciting him, and his tongue darted forward to lick the head. He toyed with it, licking and kissing it, until the big tapered dome stuck out rigid, clean of its sheath. Then Vic moved in closer, forcing it into the boy's mouth so far that Jack's nose was in the crisp, black pubic hair. Vic started to moan almost at once at how good it felt. Jack's fingers ran up and down his hairy legs. As soon as Jack touched the fellow's big nuts, his cock expanded and started to shoot, one volcanic throb after another, each throb shot a fresh stream of hot come into Jack's mouth. The taste of Vic's gism was spicy, like Ernie's had been. Jack's throat was so full of the stuff now that he could hardly swallow. Next came Brick, who Frank was urging on. "Come on," Frank's southwestern drawl was saying. "Don't cost you nothin', and everybody else is getting it. Besides, you come so darn quick, you better get rid of that easy one 'fore you try fucking that girl."

Jack desperately wanted to rest and when he saw Brick approaching him with his great thick rod. He felt like getting up and running away, except that right at his left shoulder was that big wonderful Swede that he wanted so badly. He kept his lips tightly closed when Brick started poking his cock in his face. Brick put up a threatening fist angrily. "Open up, goddamn you," he said. He was about to box Jack's ears when all of a sudden Jack felt a big gentle hand on his cheek. "Why don't you suck it, huh?" Swede's voice said, and his hand stole around the boy's face, real low, until one of his big gruff fingers found Jack's tired lips and without any more resistance, Jack parted them and let Brick put his huge thick shaft between them. This was thicker than Ernie's, not so long, but really kind of wonderful. It was so hard and so hot that his lips could feel every vein bulging out on its sides. Jack had to open his mouth wider, but Brick's didn't go in as deep as some of the others. Jack found himself enjoying it, found his tongue toying and teasing it, found his own cock was responding just as it had when Rud and Vic and Flash had done it to him. Brick was very tense about it. He'd take a couple of lone, quick jabs and then pull almost all out like he could hardly stand it. Then all of a sudden his body was trembling violently and Jack thought he'd surely drown in the explosion of rich gism that filled his mouth and throat.

Frank was waiting, his jeans rolled down, and Lon right behind him, both of them with their cocks in their hands. Frank's cock, like Frank himself, was long and thin. It's head was nicely shaped, not bigger around than its accompanying column. Jack had already decided he liked Frank, and he found sucking his big, long tool very pleasant. He was rough without being brutal, and he seemed to appreciate every stroke, whispering, "Goddamn, suck it kid, get that load," which made Jack very hot.

While Frank's was thin, he had a very smoothly muscled body. His tan skin, very pleasant to the touch, had a freshly laundered smell. Frank kept going a long time, enjoying every minute of it and making it last by letting up his deep jabs every now and then, and when he did, Jack nibbled and sucked his long rigid rod, holding his taut round ass tight, tormenting and teasing the lanky fellow until he had to plunge it in deeper.

Lon was so hot watching it that he had pulled off his clothes, keeping only his knee high lumber-jack boots on, and stood very close, getting carried away and jerking off. Jack could see his big capped dong starting to drool in excitement and he felt his own hard cock throb and throb in his pants in response. Swede stood at Jack's shoulder still, his big thigh braced against the boy's bare back, and when Jack thought he felt a gentle, big hard-on stroking the back of his neck, urging his hot mouth on to his work, he realized it was Swede's hand, and it got him so aroused he felt very close to coming, but held himself back, wanting somehow to have Swede and come at the same time Swede did. Frank's load came sudden and long, but it flowed deep into Jack's throat and didn't seem to gag him like the other's orgasm had.

The moment the tall guy backed weakly away, Lon, built wiry and smooth as a race horse, had his hard meat in Jack's mouth. After pausing for a minute with its whole length immersed in the moist fire of the boy's throat, Lon started to ride hard, so hard that Jack would have lost his balance but for Swedes support at his back. Lon was so frantic that he often pulled his big cock (not quite as big as Rud's but so super-hard that Jack loved it.) clean out of the hot, wet lips, and trying to jam it back would go wild and poke Jack's face.

Once he shot it up the boy's forehead and Jack found his lips on Lon's firm balls. With great gasping and groaning his legs spread wide apart, Lon fucked the boy's mouth relentlessly until the thick hot come began to pop out of that hard-rock tool, some of it in Jack's mouth and throat, some of it in his eyes and hair, and on his cheeks. When this was over, Jack collapsed for a couple of minutes back against Swede, who did not move. The boy panted, almost exhausted from his ordeal, but all of a sudden he became acutely conscious of the fellow standing behind him. He put out one arm, looked up at Swede's impassive, down-turned face. "Come on with me," said Swede, and led him to the back room.

Swede snatched his clothes off and shoved Jack onto one of the bunks. It was dark, but Jack, sitting on the edge of the bed, felt Swede's long hard body, his tightly muscled ass and thighs, his smooth hairy chest, his cock a huge column wedged tightly against him. As Swede's strong arms grabbed the boy close, gradually the light from the other room became sufficient for Jack to see him as well as feel him standing there, pressing his hard cock—longer and thicker even than Ernie's—against Jack's panting face. Swede held his head with one big hand.

"Can I suck it awhile?" the boy asked, and Swede's answer was to guide his big, unruly prong with one hand into the boy's mouth. Jack felt the hot tip of its great bulging head poised there a moment between his lips, and then a gentle forward thrust until almost all of its smooth broad length was imbedded deep in the boy's throat. In and out, in and out, Swede flashed it. Finally he withdrew it and knelt on the edge of the bed.

"Suck my balls," he ordered, and Jack obeyed, stroking the huge cock, slick with saliva, as he did. His tongue lapping at the big firm bag tight with pressure of the two hard balls inside, was knocking the big man out. Swede's skin was smooth as velvet over his taut muscles, and the crisp curly pubic hair excited Jack's touch so that he ripped open his jeans and let his tortured cock go free. "Suck my ass." The whispered command was accompanied with the pressure of Swede's hand on Jack's head, forcing the boy's lips to where he'd have to suck or stop breathing, and Jack sucked while Swede moaned in ecstasy. His lips kissed and lapped all around the tight hole between Swede's contracted cheeks, his tongue pushed up the hole as far as it could go, making the big blond's body writhe and his moans come clearer. Then he sucked and tongued at the same time. Jack's own cock was so hot he was afraid to touch it for fear of shooting his wad. "All right, now you're gonna get fucked," Swede said, and after letting Jack take a few more deep sucks on his huge tool, he quickly yanked the boy's body into position and inserted his immense cock into Jack's tiny little ass.

It was more than the boy had ever taken, but he was fairly used to Ernie's big cock, and while Swede's was a good deal thicker, it was only an inch of so longer, and gradually without a great deal of pain, Swede worked it in. Jack cooperated patiently, even working himself back onto it until at last it had slid home and Swede's balls crushed against the boy's firm cheeks. He started the fucking very slowly, whispering how good it felt, and Jack loved the feel of it, savored every minute of those big strong arms around him, that low voice in his ear, the gradual increase of the action. There was a shadow at the door and suddenly Swede stopped his plunging motion into Jack's hot little ass. On the bunk across the way, a tall naked figure plummeted face down and lay there inert. After about a minute, with Jack feeling Swede's big satisfying cock throbbing and throbbing deep in his behind, the boy started to twitch and squeeze and squirm about ever so little to get the big fellow in action again.

"Who's that?" Swede whispered into Jack's ear.

"It's Ernie, my buddy, the guy who was fucking Miss G. The son of a bitch must have passed clean out."

"Hell," answered Swede, "he came three times, one after another, and that was his first fuck."

"Shit, Ernie's fucked me five times in a row lots of times, and come back hot for more."

"Yeah? He been fucking you long like that?"

"About a year. And I been fucking him. I fucked him first. Rud used to do it to me."

"Hmm. I'd like to fuck that kid myself."

"Why don't you, and hurt him like he hurts me."

"You been sucking him, too?"

"No; that is, not till just the other day, and then I just hardly got the end of it in my mouth. Tonight's the first time I ever really sucked cock. I didn't think I'd like that, but damn, I sure got it tonight. When some guy grabs you and sticks it way in you, you think you're gonna choke, but you don't, and to tell the truth, it got me so fucking hot I liked it."

"Rud fucked me once when he first joined the team."

"No kiddin? Why'd you let him?"

"I wanted him to. He was so drunk, I'll bet he doesn't even remember."

"Well, I'll be damned," Jack said.

"I'll say you will," Swede's voice trembled. "I've been looking for a little cocksucker like you; one I could fuck in the ass. The hottest thing I ever saw in my life was you sucking cock after cock tonight. I damned near came off in my pants, just watching you."

"Jesus," was all Jack could answer.

"You know what we're gonna do? Get dressed and take your buddy down with us to my place and I'm gonna fuck him for you, and I'm gonna suck you both and get both of you to fuck me all weekend."

"Oh God. That'd be wonderful. Will you?"

Swede went on plunging deeper all the time. Jack, being ridden as slowly Swede, seeing that Ernie didn't move a muscle, got back into the hot rhythm, really plowing with all his hot might.

Swede and Jack dressed up, helped Ernie to dress also; the boy was so weak after his three fucks on Miss G. When they headed toward the door they gave a look toward the bed and saw Miss G. being laid by two boys, one in front, and the other in her ass. She was also sucking Rud. They saw Frank and Vic fighting to know which was going to lay her first; when the trio passed the floor they gave as excuse that they were going to go and get some whiskey.

"You know, you're queer, Jack," Swede went on. "Just like me, and you and I are gonna team up, kid. You're gonna be the queerest fucking queen that ever lived, next to me. You're gonna fuck and suck and get fucked by all the soldiers, truck drivers, ball players, lumberjacks, and farm boys in this state...."

PART TWO
HOMOSEXUALITY
AND THE MILITARY

Because these stories usually find a good market among military men on leave, many authors have centered their stories in military locales and with military personnel. Many a lonely soldier or sailor has purchased stories such as these so that they could help wile away his long evenings as C.Q. or Sergeant of the guard. Of course the stories contained herein are directed to homosexual sailors, soldiers and/or marines. However, the majority of such storied dealing with the military generally are heterosexually oriented.

Of the stories contained in this chapter, the first, *My Assignment*, was the most unique due to the fact that in its original form each page was very carefully illustrated, graphically depicting the people and actions of the story. This is not particularly unusual in this type literature. Very often many months, sometimes years, are devoted to the preparation of the stencil from which the "Tijuana Bibles" are produced. Painstaking labor is put into the sketches, and talented artists are paid well to exhibit their skills. Naturally the fully illustrated versions of the short stories command a very handsome price. Whereas the ordinary mimeographed story usually sells for anywhere from one dollar to twenty-five dollars—the fully illustrated version sells for three and four times that.

One Night on a Beach, Crowded Hotel, Bill and the Sailor, Bail Out, as well as *My Assignment*, are all excellent examples of the type of erotic literature that was being circulated during World War II.

Men in uniform hold an undeniable attraction for most everyone. As Dr. Alfred Kinsey stated, the public is much more conscious of the behavior of a man in uniform than it is of a man in civilian clothes. It is for this very reason that the "Tijuana Bible" stories which deal with sexual experiences of military personnel are in demand. Insofar as homosexuality in the armed forces is concerned, again referring to a statement by Dr. Kinsey, "there is a ready assumption that men in segregated groups, as in the Army and the Navy, turn to the homosexual more often than they would at home."

It is necessary that one be (or have been) a member of the armed forces in order to understand the attitudes which prevail amongst the men therein as concerns matters sexual. One military man does not like to think that his buddy is "queer", but if they happen to get a little high together and wind up their evening by participating in a mutually satisfying homosexual relationship (as innocent possibly as simple mutual masturbation) no great deal of importance is placed upon the incident. Many of the men openly discuss how drunk and "kiddish" they had acted the night before.

The military Y.M.C.A.'s across the country are very popular as spas wherein military men can openly enjoy their homosexuality. It is in places such as these that the service man will find the restricting atmosphere of barracks life, the regimentation of a military system which he has been accustomed to, but at the same time he finds the freedom to satisfy his homosexual urges.

CHAPTER THREE
MY ASSIGNMENT

The old Army bus groaned its bumpy way the last few miles to the small communications building located in a secluded section of the Mojave Desert. Assignment to "Out-House" meant a physical isolation from the outside world. I would bring the Army installation to full strength. Grand total: Seven. Our mission was to process data taken by and transmitted from certain secret satellites which our government seemed to be sending heavenward at a prodigious rate. The rickety old bus moved slowly on into the moonless night and, coupled with monotonous scenery, made for a pretty dull ride. I dozed a little until the bus lurched to a stop and I was deposited at my destination. The driver waited just long enough for me to secure my gear, then, clouding the placid atmosphere with billowing dust clouds, headed back to the Air Force base. The building was a low-slung concrete structure, plain, austere and typically military. With duffle bag on my shoulder and the overnight case in hand, I trudged up the white gravel walkway. The door was open. Grayly silhouetted in its frame, a shirtless figure stood leaning against the jamb.

"Welcome to Out-House!" he said, opening the screen door.

"Thanks," I said, struggling through the door. The room was illuminated only by the silvery white light of a television set around which sprawled the other five soldiers. All were comfortably but skimpily dressed for the very warm dry evening.

"I'm Jerry Lowe," the tall well-built kid drawled, "the first

'Louie' in charge."

Not knowing whether to salute this husky youth clad only in tight Levi's, I instead offered my hand. "Jon Jacobson." Jerry's grip was firm as he took my extended hand.

"You're just in time to catch the feature movie. Hey Ed, take Jon and show him his bunk."

Travel weary, I declined the television offer in order to shower and hit the sack.

The next morning I was awakened by a gentle roll of the bunk and gradually focused my eyes upon a flock of flaming red hair perched atop a handsome freckled face in which a pair of pale blue eyes squinted down at me.

"Time to rise and shine." Memory flooded back to me: it was my roommate, Ed.

At breakfast, I met the rest of the group. There was Ron Blake. A handsome fellow about my height with blue-black hair and the olive complexion of an Italian. Swede, as his name implies, was a husky blond that could easily play fullback for the pros. Sandy-haired Dick was the youngest and also the smallest of the group, standing about five four. Frank and Don had medium builds, but in their own way, were good-looking kids.

Breakfast was uneventful. The day began quietly enough. About ten o'clock, the radio informed us of new launchings. Both Army and Air Force were at it! Our little center sprang into immediate action.

Those first few weeks flew by. Eventually all three services had launched several secret satellites and all of them relayed an unbelievable amount of data. We worked practically around the clock, up to twenty hours a day. The military aspect of the duty was practically nonexistent, but our shifts were long and arduous.

Because of the searing heat, we dressed only in our most comfortable clothes. For the most part that meant summer shorts and sometimes a loose shirt. From time to time I would have a moment free coinciding with one or two of the others, and we were able to become somewhat acquainted. I only saw

Ed in the mornings for a few minutes, and occasionally Ron and Swede who were right across the hall. I probably saw them the most. Our hours were very similar, but after working those long hours, no one was in the mood for long chats. Our work continued at this crazy pace with no letup for six weeks. Then, just as suddenly as it had begun, our jobs were finished for a while.

Vandenburg had all the information it needed.

That first night of relaxation was quiet. Everyone just seemed to collapse. We couldn't leave the installation for forty-eight hours in case more data would be required. So there we remained, isolated out there in the blistering California desert heat. Our first day off was spent in a leisurely fashion. Some caught up on correspondence. We all did the menial chores of washing, cleaning rooms. In the early evening a few went for short hikes, several played games, and Dick and I got in a few sets of tennis. Dick wore just some short shorts and I cut the legs off a pair of Levi's in the fashion of the rest of the group.

We all gathered that evening in front of the TV set. I had the uneasy feeling that everyone was behaving in a restrained manner, acting much like a couple chaperoned on a date—I finally attributed the general silence to sheer physical exhaustion. I felt somehow as if I really hadn't been accepted fully into the group. Thoughts wandered through my mind rather haphazardly, and I dozed off and on through a rather lengthy and prosaic movie. I shut my eyes, just listening to the sound. When I opened them at the movie's conclusion, the room was dark.

The light of the full moon filtered through the windows. I looked over at Dick on the floor. His fly was wide open and someone, I couldn't recognize who, was running his hands over Dick's smooth body. His head moved down Dick's flat stomach and I could see this tongue lightly caress Dick from his neck to the hair in his crotch. The other guy slid his hands inside Dick's pants and pushed them down around Dick's knees, exposing a throbbing prick. Red hair glistened in the moonlight; the other guy was Ed!

Ed quickly took Dick's hard-on into his mouth. Dick then reached down and unfastened Ed's bulging Levi's. What a cock! I can't remember seeing one larger. As soon as Ed dropped to his knees and French-kissed Dick, Ed was sucking ardently. I could see Dick's chest heave and fall in thrilled passionate breaths. Then Dick reached for Ed's throbbing tool. Twisting around he found Ed's seeping prick. Plunging the enormous rod into his mouth as far as he could, he lunged forward and Ed's slippery tool dug deeply down Dick's throat. Ed groaned in delight. Jerry meanwhile moistened Ed's tail hole with a darting tongue, then lay behind Ed. He slowly inserted his own throbbing cock where his tongue had been delicious moments before. The three of them thus entangled, their fiery passions unified and blazing, pulsated in unison. It was a pretty picture and I was becoming very excited.

Suddenly, groans from the other side of the room caught my attention. Frank, Ron and Swede were nude. They alternated kissing and sucking each other. Frank and Ron got into a sixty-nine position. Swede ran his tongue between their crevices. Swede finally dissuaded Frank from Ron's swollen cock and Frank then went to town on Swede. Swede drank Ron's juices, and Ron, Frank's, but Swede got up, walked to the other side of the room. Jerry, who had just flushed Ed's ass with his hot come, rested. Ed said to Swede, "Shove it to me you blond fucking bastard."

Very shortly after that, Dick and Ed reached what I could tell was a tremendous climax. As Swede's long thick cock found Ed's hole, I unbuttoned my pants freeing my cramped erection. The Swede's swelling prick was hurting Ed, and by this time Swede had Jerry's cock in his mouth. Then Ron rolled over and tickled Swede's legs with his tongue. I watched avidly as Ron's tongue moved higher, higher, higher, higher until it found the Swede's asshole. The Swede soon reached a climax and he writhed in blissful ecstasy when Jerry, too, shot his sweet warm load. Tension rose within me. As I was discreetly massaging my stiff, seeping cock, running my hand loosely up and down the solid firm tool, someone of the group got up and walked into the kitchen. I didn't notice him return. Suddenly, there was a bright light shining into my face! He had gotten a flashlight! Instantly I was frightened. He swung a fist at me! I ducked, the blow grazing my shoulder. In that instant I awoke with a start. The Swede was standing over me and his hand rested lightly on my shoulder. "Easy boy," he said calmly. "You must have been having a hell of a nightmare."

My whole body shook. I looked around the room, bewildered. The others were doing the same thing that they had been when I dozed off. I got up, mumbled a half-hearted "thanks," and walked out of the room, going to the kitchen for a cup of coffee and a cigarette. Frank suggested we play hearts I was agreeable since I wasn't ready to go to bed, jittery as I was. The game of cards went by uneventfully but most enjoyable and everyone for the first time seemed to be thoroughly relaxed. On our third game, I relaxed enough to notice the bulging pants of all these desirable lads seated as we were on the floor with crossed legs. I began to feel uneasy with tension again rising within me. I threw in my hand and went to bed. It's hell to be so horny! That was my last thought before I slumbered.

* * * * * * *

The next morning I jumped into a pair of cut off Levi's and sleepily ambled out to the kitchen for that badly needed first cup of coffee. The sun was already very bright. It was going to be a warm day and it was only nine-thirty. Ron Blake, his curly black hair disheveled, was just sitting down at the table across from Dick. Both were in their shorts. My eyes didn't miss the open slot of Ron's boxer shorts, and I began to feel a little melancholy.

"Good morning. Ron, Dick," I attempted cheerfulness.

Dick got up, "How 'bout some eggs?"

"No thanks." Dick's jockey shorts fit snugly. His small muscular ass flexed invitingly with every step he took. His large, soft prick, imprisoned by the white shorts which outlined the circumcised head, bounced buoyantly upon a large pair of balls. The sight of his tight molded form made me shake with what I like to term frustration nerves. "Where's everybody?" I queried.

"The gang went into town for a couple of days. It's Dick's and my turn to hold down the fort," Ron said with flat nonchalance between sips of coffee.

"You're free to go to town, too, if you want."

"Don't know how I'd get there. Anyway, I've got plenty of correspondence to catch up on."

I decided what I needed most was in town, but I couldn't get there. The second best thing to do, I figured, would be some physical exercise. I dressed quickly after breakfast, then proceeded to take a long hike. Despite the heat, the day was beautiful. It was the first opportunity I had had to explore the surrounding desert since coming to "OUT-HOUSE." It was late afternoon before I tired sufficiently to head back. Tired, hot and hungry, I got back to the building at four-thirty. I showered and cleaned off the fine desert dust from my boots. After finishing several personal chores, I realized that I hadn't seen either Ron or Dick since I returned. I climbed into a clean pair of boxer shorts and headed for Ron's room. Ron wasn't there, so I trundled on down the hall to see if Dick was in. The door was half open. Without bothering to knock or announce my presence, I stuck my head into the room. I was stunned!

Both were asleep. Ron was laying on his back naked. Dick was lying between Ron's legs with his head on Ron's stomach, his hand tightly grasping Ron's semi-stiff cock. What I wouldn't have given for a Polaroid! The light patches of dark hair on Ron's chest and stomach, and Dick's almost hairless body...both bodies in such a tender position...my heart kindly went out to them. I went to the kitchen to make some iced coffee. Filling a small tray with three tall glasses, cream and sugar, I headed back to Dick's room. Ron woke with a start as I gingerly placed the tray on the stand beside the bed.

"Coffee?" I said smiling. Ron's face displayed a confused expression.

"Sure," he replied quietly.

Dick stirred a little. Not realizing I was there and without opening his eyes, he moved his head down to gently kiss Ron's awakening cock, slipping it in his mouth with familiarity.

"How 'bout some iced coffee, Dick?" Ron firmly voiced.

Dick sat up with a quick startled movement. Ron gently but firmly pulled him back down against him. I broke a strained silence. "Are you lovers or was this just for fun?"

"Damn!" Dick said finally, adding, "we've been lovers since the first week we arrived here. I met Ron at basic training and fortunately, we were both stationed here."

"Now at least I'll have a couple of people to talk freely to occasionally. Or maybe even borrow a few bobbie pins." They laughed a tension relaxing guffaw. From that moment on we were good friends. Dick jumped up and pulled on his pants.

"We've a friend coming for dinner tonight, so I'd better get things started." Dick stood up and before dashing off to the kitchen, he lightly kissed me. I was, needless to say, pleasantly surprised.

Not too long after the sun had set, a Chevy drove up. Ron and Dick went out to meet their friend. A boring evening, I anticipated, would be spent entertaining their straight friend. Dick introduced me to David, a handsome boy about twenty, dishwater-blond, with intriguing hazel eyes. David had such an amiable personality and was such a stimulating conversation-alist, that the evening really flew by.

The beer we'd been drinking all evening swelled my bladder uncomfortably until I was forced to excuse myself and go to the head for a piss. I hated to tear myself away from the engaging chatter.

Returning from the john down the darkened hall, the only light filtering through from the dimly lit lounge, Dave met me, evidently on his way to the head also. For an instant our eyes locked. It gave me the shivers; I felt an urge to kiss his dark red lips. He asked for a light. As I held the lighter up to his cigarette, his hand held mine softly and he gave me a gentle squeeze when it was lit. I looked at him for a moment, then without really thinking, grabbed him by the back of the neck and kissed him. His arms reached around me, pulling me close to him. He held me warmly, tightly, and I could feel the solid bulge swell, though confined tightly by continental pants. My heart began racing, my own cock hardening. As we disengaged, I asked, "How about another drink?"

"Sounds good, after I take a piss," he said, giving me a firm squeeze and a sly wink.

I waited while he took a leak, then we walked out to join Ron and Dick. Ron and Dick had placed fresh drinks and sandwiches on the coffee table in front of the divan. The front door was open, letting in the cool breeze that helped to refresh us as well as air out the smoke-filled room. Dave sat in the center of the couch and I sat on his right. Ron and Dick were on the floor at opposite ends of the table.

The conversation resumed, wandering freely, though a trifle animated, from current politics to the pennant races.

Imperceptibly, Dave's knee found mine, which he proceeded to delicately rub ever so slowly up and down. Our snack consumed, we sat back against the couch. Dave lifted his arm, placing it on top of the couch's back, his hand behind my head. I found it difficult to concentrate on the various topics. Slowly Dave's hand lightly touched my neck. Soon the gentle massage of his strong warm hand relaxed my taut neck and shoulder muscles. My free hand rested lightly on his knee.

As I did so, a tingling sensation crept through my crotch. Dick helped Rod clear the dirty dishes from in front of us. They had hardly disappeared from view when Dave leaned over and kissed me. His lips were warm; his tongue played tenderly between my closed lips. Emotions kindled my insides and I gently pushed him away, saying, "You're staying in my room tonight."

Just at that moment, before Dave had the chance to reply—for

I really didn't know if he had intended to stay the evening—Ron and Dick returned. Ron suggested Dave spend the night since it was already so late. I offered Dave the use of my toiletries, adding that he could use Ed's available bunk. All agreeing, we turned in for the night.

In my room, Dave lit a cigarette. He stood looking at me for a long moment. His gaze flowed up and down as though he had X-ray vision. My cheeks crimsoned. Putting his cigarette out, he moved toward me to grasp me between his powerful arms. Meeting my almost hypnotic hazel gaze, he whispered, "Hi," intimately before embracing me. I pulled him down onto the bed, our lips locking passionately. This time I parted my lips to his eager tongue which darted in and out exploring my oral crevice. We held one another tightly. My emotions fired to the point, I was shaking with excitement and anticipation.

Slowly, tantalizingly, he unbuttoned my shirt until his warm hand stroked my hairless chest and stomach. I pulled his shirt free of his now bulging trousers and pulled it up around his chest, baring his slim stomach. With a slight push, he lay back against the bed. I buried my head against his belly, kissing, licking and gently biting. Cupping my head in his hands, he leaned over and caressed my hungry lips. When I rubbed his smooth back, his muscles rippled. And then I pulled off his shirt. Setting him up on the edge of the bed, I quickly removed his shoes and fought his zipper. Opening his pants, I pressed my lips to the throbbing bulge in his shorts and blew warm air on his heavy prick. Then spreading the elastic band and freeing his large dripping cock, my lips snaked over it until I could feel his balls against my chin and my nose pressed tightly into his abdomen.

Short seconds later we were disrobed and tightly entwined. His tongue and hot moist breath played excitedly in my ear. Slowly he moved down. First around my neck, then to the nipples, then his tongue found my belly button. I quivered with emotion. Down further his tongue ran over the inside of my thighs until he chewed at the juncture of leg and abdomen, his cheek pressed against my hairy balls. Finally I released an agonizing sigh as his lips and tongue caressed my cock, aching with anticipation.

With one quick movement, my throbbing, seeping cock was in his hot mouth, Dave's tongue working magically on the underside as he slowly moved up and down its full length. I had to have his prick in my mouth, so he swung his legs up to my head, then we coupled. The excitement heightened to an almost unbearable pitch as we slowly worked on each other's cock. Getting too close to a climax, I pulled my hot tool from his mouth. He took to licking my crotch, as I was doing to him. His flesh tasted clean if a trifle salty. Shortly we found each other's quivering ass hole. My tongue ripped into his secret crevice while he passionately tongued mine, we again took each other's cock and sucked with wild abandonment. With a moan, Dave began to quiver excitedly just about the same time I began writhing. His load, hot, sweet, plentiful, flooded my mouth and I pressed forward to shove it down my throat. My come shot hard and he greedily drank every drop.

We lay there, our heads resting on each other's thighs, exhausted. I found the pillow which had fallen on the floor. We embraced tenderly, then tightly entangled but comfortable, and with our bodies pressing each other at every conceivable point we slept.

CHAPTER FOUR
ONE NIGHT ON A BEACH

At one time during my stay in Africa, I was stationed at what had once been a very fashionable summer resort. Because the weather was terrifically hot most of the time we were there, it wasn't unusual to spend most of our time in the sea, and the usual manner of swimming was in the nude since there was little danger of any female coming around. It was strictly a male's paradise. Many an afternoon I sat on the porch of the library, watching nude bathers through a pair of binoculars borrowed from a friend. There was every conceivable kind of prick there, and they were all usually in various degrees of hardness. The really interesting sight was to watch those who had already had their swim and were sunning; lying there on the beach in complete abandon. Every once in a while a prick would slowly start to rise, its owner probably dreaming of better times, and soon it would be standing upright, straight as a pole. Then the kidding would start. Some of them were lovely poles and provoked daydreams of how wonderful it would feel to have that hard pole in one's mouth, and to caress it with one's lips and tongue. Sometimes I wondered, if it was all kidding, for one day two beautiful men were fooling around rather close to the library. They both had terrific hard-ons, but one had a larger pole which the other was trying to get stuck up his ass; once or twice it got stuck in far enough that I didn't think they were pretending. The other fellows on the beach were having a good laugh over the performance while I sat there with a pulsing prick that could do nothing but pulse.

That evening as it was getting dark, I went for a swim down the beach, a short distance from the quarters, which were now occupied by only a few British flying officers. I shed all my clothes and waded out into the water. I couldn't swim, but the water was cool and felt wonderful after the heat of the day. After fifteen minutes of splashing around and thinking over the sights of the afternoon, I noticed I was not alone. I could see someone swimming farther out in the sea toward a sandbar which was a favorite resting place. Since I couldn't wade out that far, I went back to the beach and I lay down on my towel. I never got back into the water that night, for in about ten minutes I heard the swimmer approaching the shore. I raised up on my elbows and saw a rather huge figure wading in to shore and heading straight toward where I lay. I didn't know whether to get up and leave, but decided to stay there and see what happened. When he came closer I could see he had also not worn any shorts. He walked over and dropped down beside me without any hesitation and began talking with me. I learned he was one of the British flying officers stationed in the Villa behind us, and he never went swimming except at night, for he hated to wear trunks and didn't like to go swimming nude in front of everybody on the beach.

We talked for some time as I was lying on my back, and he was resting on one elbow looking down into my face, my prick was having a very hard time not to rare up without ado, but I managed to keep it halfway soft while trying to see his in the meantime. There was only a little moonlight, but I managed to get a pretty definite idea of his shape and looks, which were both exciting. He smelled fresh and wet, very masculine, and I could sec vaguely that he was well hung. I was certain it was far from soft, so I let myself go and my dick really got hard.

* * * * * * *

I noticed several times that he was looking me over from

head to toe, and would pause momentarily when he got to the regions of my now pulsating dick. Finally I switched the conversation to Picadilly Circus, Cafe Royale, and a few other choice spots around London, so he would have no doubt as to what I expected. I also talked about Oscar Wilde to clinch my argument.

It was exactly what he had been waiting for, since I could see his dick begin to swell with anticipation. I rolled on my side and up onto my elbow so that my prick was pointing directly at his now rigid pole. I suggested he share my towel with me, since he would be getting sand all over him lying on the beach. He said he would wash the sand off first and then lie down, as he went into the water. When he came back he dropped down beside me, and since the towel wasn't large enough to hold us both unless we were close together, he was right up against me.

As he laid down, our hard pricks came together for a second and then his arms went around me pulling me close into a warm embrace. Our lips came together in a very passionate kiss; he drew my tongue into his warm mouth and sucked on it, and when he was through I eagerly sucked on his, crushing his exciting body against mine. His huge prick was throbbing against my thighs and mine rested between our stomachs. That first kiss lasted a long time, as we held each other with one arm and let the other wander caressingly over each other's backs, down across the ass to the hair surrounding our pricks. Finally we held each other's throbbing prick in our hands.

He took his lips from mine and suggested it would be better to go to his room, and explained he slept alone and had a portable cot. It would be much safer than being out here on the beach, and I readily agreed. We walked over to the Villa with our towels wrapped around us. It was very dark so he took my hand and led me up the stairs to his room, locking the door once we were inside. I dropped my clothes into a chair, and once more he took me into his arms, practically smothering me with kisses. His hand undid my towel and it fell to the floor, and we stood there naked, everything revealed and throbbing for action.

I thought we might double up on the cot, but he had a better idea and took all the blankets off the cot, spreading them on the floor to make a very comfortable pallet. He got another towel, washcloth, pan of water, a tube of Vaseline, and came back to me on the pallet. I lay on my back with my hard prick sticking straight up, and he washed me very gently around the balls, between my legs, the hair around my prick and then my throbbing prick itself, until all the sea water had been washed away. Then he washed himself and laid down, taking me into his strong arms immediately.

He placed his lovely cock between my legs, which I squeezed as tightly as I could to imprison it there. My cock lay against his stomach so that when he began moving his cock in and out between my legs the action also began rubbing my prick against his stomach. We began kissing again, and he let his tongue flip easily into my mouth and I began sucking it as it probed the inner recesses of my throat. Then he began a few short pushes between my legs with his prick, and I could feel the hot, naked head of his dong caressing the cheeks of my ass with every thrust. Soon his prick was throbbing violently, so he rose on his arms while I rolled over on my stomach. He was still astride me, and raising up on his knees, he reached for the Vaseline and began to grease my ass with it. He then greased his prick, pulling the skin back as far as it would go and greasing every inch of it back down to his stomach. I lay there eagerly awaiting the entry of the lovely prick into my ass, and to have every inch of it stuck into me.

While I held the cheeks of my ass apart, he started to very gently ease it in. With all the greasing and the browning I had done recently, he had no trouble slipping it in. He had about nine inches of slender cock, a perfect tool for fucking, and he had a wonderful technique. He began slowly pushing it in as far as it would go, letting his lovely balls jiggle against my ass each time. When he felt it was sliding back and forth with sufficient ease for a really good fuck, he lowered himself down on my back, grasping my cock with one hand and my balls with the other. This made me raise my ass up to meet his every thrust, so he could drive his cock into me to the very last inch. He began going up and down, in and out of my asshole with a rhythmic motion that had anything beat for smoothness that I had ever met in my life. Even when it came time for him to shoot his load, he was still going smoothly. Perhaps the amount of Vaseline helped the smoothness, but it was the least painful and most exciting fucking I had ever had. He was jerking me off at the same time, also using a smooth stroke, and just as he began to shoot his own nuts, he gave one mighty pull and yanked down on my prick and I also shot my load. I squeezed my cheeks together to hold that lovely prong in me as long as I could, and just lay there enjoying the feeling of his hot prick filling my ass. When it softened, he pulled it out and I turned over on the blanket. He washed our pricks off and then the Vaseline off my ass, which still felt good from his fucking.

We lay down and began kissing again. He kissed my eyes, nose, mouth and then began kissing my chest, letting his tongue and teeth caress my tits. With treatment like this it didn't take long before my prick was straight as a ramrod again. He kept on tonguing and kissing my body, slowly moving down to the navel, letting his tongue grope searchingly into it. Soon he was down to my prick and his lips and tongue lovingly began to caress the head of it and to slide gently up and down the entire shaft. He tongued the slit and sucked gently on the head, gradually turning his body and bringing his own prick up to my face. I turned on my side and eagerly began to kiss his hard prick and tongue the head. He took my cock deep into his throat and I went down all the way on his until I could feel the hot, pulsing head of it deep in the recesses of my throat. We both began to suck vigorously, slowly at first, and then faster as the eagerness to taste each other's cream became almost unbearable. Our tongues slid down the rigid shafts, and our noses rested in pubic hair. Then we began sucking with everything we had, wrapping our arms around each other's ass, finger fucking as we sucked. Our loads shot at just about the same time and he filled my mouth with the sweet come I wanted so badly. He raised his mouth to mine and we kissed, exchanging a little of each other's juice and swallowed.

We laid there for over an hour resting and letting our hands roam over each other's body at will. Since bed check was at 11:00, I arose and dressed. The next day I saw him out drilling his men, and saluted as I passed. He smiled and winked, and pointed to the beach letting me know he would meet me there again tonight. There were many such pleasure-filled nights for the next two months until I was transferred. He never did learn my identity, but I know his as he is now a famous officer commanding an army that may determine the fate of India.

CHAPTER FIVE
CROWDED HOTEL

Bill breathed a heavy sigh of relief as he let himself into the hotel room and dropped his suitcase on the floor. Gosh, but New York was crowded on the holiday weekend, he thought. He had been to three hotels that evening and having found them all full, had finally taken a double room in desperation with the words of the roomclerk still ringing in his ears, "I may have to put someone else in with you—awfully crowded over the holidays, you know."

Well, for the time being, he was alone and the solitude was indeed welcome. This was his first furlough in three months, and the cramped barrack's living was beginning to grate on his nerves. He made it to New York from Camp Le Jeune in only eleven hours of driving, and he was exhausted. Kicking off his shoes, he dropped onto the large double bed and stretched out his long frame. Ye Gods but he was tired! He probably could sleep a month, but that was scarcely why he had made the long trip to the big city. No, there would probably be precious little sleep for him this weekend.

With a tired yawn, he stood up and began stripping off his uniform. It had become somewhat wrinkled from the long trip, but a few hours of hanging in the closet and it would be as good as new again. He hung his jacket, shirt and pants all very carefully, and as he pulled off his undershirt, he found himself standing before a full length mirror hinged to the closet door. Smiling back at him from the mirror was a magnificent figure of a man and, although Bill had probably never heard of Narcissus, he couldn't help but admire himself.

His curly, chestnut brown hair tumbled over his brow and almost into his deep brown eyes. His finely chiseled features were those of a Grecian statue while his body improved on the art of ancient Greeks. His thick neck rose proudly from his massive shoulders, and his wrists and forearms were magnificently formed while his upper arms trembled with latent power as he flexed them. The rigid muscles of his abdominal arch and hip radiated virile masculinity, and his perfectly formed thighs and calves completed a picture of powerful and vibrant creation. As he dropped his shorts, his sexual organ was displayed; it was six inches long in a limp state and when excited, rose to ten inches. His balls were large and beautifully formed, and completed this picture of virile manhood.

Bill stood admiring himself thusly for some time before stepping into the adjoining shower room where he enjoyed the luxury of a shower, he walked back into the bedroom and, turning on the bed-light, he crawled between the crisp white sheets. This was sheer paradise, he thought, as he picked up a magazine from the bedside table and began to read.

He had not read more than a page when he heard someone fumbling at the door; it opened, and in walked the nicest, tall blond sailor. "Excuse me," he said, "the desk clerk told me that the room was half sold already, but he didn't know whether or not you had gone out."

"Perfectly okay," said Bill, "come on in and make yourself at home. Here, let me help you with your luggage." With that, Bill climbed out of the bed and picked up the sailor's heavy duffel bag and set it in the closet.

"Thanks," said the sailor. "By the way, the name's Jerry Waters."

"Bill Longstreet's mine. A real pleasure to know you, Jerry."

They shook hands and Bill was pleased at Jerry's firm clasp. As the sailor's eyes moved up and down over Bill's body, he suddenly realized that he was completely naked, but the sailor's frank admiration pleased him, so he strolled casually back to the bed as he said, "The management wishes to accommodate and cater to every desire. There's a sensational shower through that door, I recommend it highly."

"Thanks," laughed the sailor, "I'll follow your recommendation to the letter." And with that, he began peeling off his blue middy and the body of the handsome creature was slowly revealed. Bill could not help but stare in admiration, as Jerry was even more perfectly built than himself. As the sailor pulled off his T-shirt, the muscles of his shoulders and arms glistened in the overhead light, the shadows accenting his deeply muscled chest. Turning around, he dropped his shorts and Bill admired the sailor's tight buttocks and magnificent legs. As Jerry turned to face the bed, Bill could scarcely suppress a gasp of surprise, as this lad was more superbly equipped sexually than himself. Hanging between his legs was a full eight inches of limp penis. The sailor's body tapering from broad shoulders to slim, well-muscled waist and hip, was truly perfection in masculine physique.

"Be back in a minute," he called, as he moved into the shower; his muscles rippling as he walked, like some jungle creature.

Bill tried to return to his reading but found his attention continually wandering to the shower door, behind which the steady stream of water almost drowned out the occupant's noises in washing. Bill was severely tempted to join his room-mate's activity in the shower, but the water stopped and shortly the glistening body of the sailor walked through the door into the bedroom.

"How was it?"

"Terrific. I feel like a million," was the reply, as the sailor finished drying his curly blond hair. Tossing the towel on a chair, he walked over and sat down on the edge of the bed.

It was a warm evening and Bill lay propped up on a pillow, covered only by a sheet to his waist. His eyes traveled over the sailor's broad shoulder, the abdominal wall, the chest packed firm and hard. Yet always he returned to the muscular thighs and loins. Bill took in every detail of the boy as there was something about Jerry, something about the smell of him, something insidious about his magnetism that was inciting. It was there in the sailor's glistening blond hair, it was in his ripe and sensuous lips, in the expanse of his broad chest, his narrow hips and buttocks, his rounded kneecaps and calves; and Bill was almost sick because the ferment in his loins was so strong.

Bill was suddenly conscious of the sailor's stare and realized he had been asked a question. "Excuse me, Jerry, I was thinking of something else."

"Who is she?" grinned the sailor, indicating the huge bulge in the sheet where Bill's erection stretched the linen taut.

Half embarrassed, Bill closed the magazine and reached for the light. "Time to hit the sack," was his only reply.

"Just a minute," and the sailor crawled over to the other side of the bed and slipped under the sheet.

"Want a blanket?"

"No, this is perfect."

"Okay, here she goes," and the light flicked out, leaving the room only dimly lit from the street far below.

Gliding down into the sheets, Bill felt his leg brush that of his roommate and he trembled at the contact. Was it only his overworked imagination, or was the pressure of his leg being returned by the sailor? Glancing to his side at the tousled head, he saw Jerry smiling at him, their faces only inches apart. Bill's arms ached, just such a short distance separated them; it would be so easy, a slight roll of his body and they would be together. The sailor's blue eyes invited, hypnotized, danced before him. Glancing down, Bill saw the enormous bulge of the sailor's cock, erect and vibrant with virility.

With a half stifled sob, Bill rolled over on his side and tossed his arm around the warm pulsating body before him. At this contact, the sailor moaned lightly and wound his arms around Bill's back drawing their bodies together, his sensuous lips parted, expectant.

They kissed—kissed deeply and hungrily—and inside Bill's

head there was a bursting of rockets and pinwheels throwing sparks against the back of his eyelids. With a surge of emotion, he pulled the sailor's body even closer and flexed his arms until their bodies were blended into one.

They finally pulled apart and Jerry opened his eyes, looked into Bill's face and said, "Oh, God," his voice husky with emotion. Bill's hands played over the sailor's chest and abdomen while Jerry's lips moved over the marines eyes, throat and shoulders. Finally Bill was stroking the sailor's penis, which had swollen to fully twelve inches and was as thick as his wrist. Inserting this monster organ between his legs, Bill began a gradual reciprocating motion which so affected the sailor that he began gripping and kneading Bills shoulders and back. Finally he gasped, "Stop!" and they once again embraced passionately.

Soon Jerry's lips began moving over Bill's body. He covered his throat and chest with hot torrid kisses and moved on to his stomach. Winding his arms around Bill's hips, Jerry let his lips glide over Bill's turgid genitals, stroking and caressing with his tongue. Bill moaned in ecstasy and stretched out. Finally the sailor inserted the entire cock in his mouth and delicately balancing the pressure between his lips and tongue, let the gigantic organ slide into his mouth. Gradually he increased the motion until Bill grasped his head and forced him to stop. "I damn near came off then," he whispered, "and I don't want to yet."

Jerry raised his head, his eyes moist, "You're—you're wonderful," he whispered, half sobbing as he wrapped his arms around Bills chest and buried his head into his shoulder.

CHAPTER SIX
BILL AND THE SAILOR

Bill lay stretched out on the sand, his tanned muscular body absorbing the rays of the mid-afternoon sun. He was alone on one of his favorite stretches of beach, a little known spot where he usually found solitude.

Today finding the beach empty, as usual, he stripped entirely and lay completely naked, his magnificent body completely exposed, revealing his broad muscular shoulders which taper to a slim hard waist and narrow hips, down to his well-filled thighs and calves. Nature had smiled upon him in another manner as well, for between his legs lay a rich endowment of virility. His organ, in a limp state, was fully seven inches long, but when erect, climbed to ten inches. As he lay basking under the hot sun, the heat tickled his flesh and brought his sexual desire and drive surging upward. Gradually his organ became hard, and when it reached its full height, he amused himself by stroking it ever so gently.

While amusing himself, he heard an embarrassed cough behind him. He turned his head and immediately sat up to take a better look. The intruder on his solitude was a tall, dark, curly-haired sailor whose handsome face was set off by an infectious grin.

"Come on in, the water's fine," Bill laughed, as he beckoned the sailor to join him.

"Don't mind if I do," was the response, and the sailor began pulling off his white middy. Bill gave a gasp of amazement as the body of the sailor was slowly revealed. First his muscled shoulders and arms appeared, above a deep, well-defined chest. His waist and hips were slim and firm as he dropped his trousers, his well-muscled legs could be seen; and as he removed his shorts, Bill could hardly believe his eyes as the boy was more superbly equipped than he was himself. Bill's eyes clung longingly on nine inches of gorgeous thick penis, dangling tantalizingly between his muscular thighs.

As the sailor stretched himself out on the sand beside him, Bill felt a warm glow course through him and could hardly restrain his voice as he asked,

"You're from SQUANTO, aren't you?"

"Thanks for guessing, you're right."

"How do you like it there?"

"Oh, it's okay, but I like it better right here, now," was the upsetting answer, and as if to emphasize his words, the sailor threw his arms around Bill's shoulders and grinned broadly into his face.

Bill moved until his leg was brushing his companion's, and turned his head slightly to get a better look at him. He had never been so intensely thrilled and excited before in his life, and as the sailor began rubbing his leg back and forth along Bill's, he could feel himself getting an erection. He made no move to hide it, but let it grow, feeling bolder every minute. The sailor's hand was gripping his shoulder tightly now and Bill, glancing down, saw a sight that left him limp and shaking with excitement. The sailor had an erection fully twelve inches long and almost as thick as his wrist. Bill gasped audibly and stared up into the sailor's eyes, and the sailor fully understood the significance of the look. Pulling slightly, he drew Bill to him and within a moment had both arms locked behind his back. Bill parted his lips slightly, closed his eyes, and felt the sailor's lips upon his own. Bill wrapped his arms around the boy's body and pressed him to him. They lay for fully five minutes in this position, finally separating, and began to fondle each other's body. Bill was fascinated by the size of the sailor's cock and bending over, took it between his lips. The sailor moaned slightly and stretched his frame out. Bill began moving his lips across the enormous prong and finally inserted the entire thing into his mouth.

Moving up and down with increasing speed, the sailor began to become very excited, and gripped Bill's head with both hands and pushed in rhythm.

CHAPTER SEVEN
BAIL OUT

Gasping for breath, he pulled the cord as the knife-like sensation of falling spiraled through his body. Time stopped, and an eternity later a sudden pull jolted him into consciousness again. He swayed from side to side as the parachute billowed above him. He seemed to have stopped falling and to be suspended in air.

He saw the dying PBY drunkenly glide toward the water. As he looked, the flaming nose pointed downward, and in an instant the plane was beneath the waves. He shuddered, wondering how many of his buddies had died in that instant. Then he saw the other parachutes. There were two of them. *Only three of us,* he thought. *Three out of seven.*

The swaying bodies were too far away from him to identify them. The waves below were coming up fast. He looked around then and spotted the emergency kit he had pushed out as he jumped. He figured he would come down just west of it. The gray-blue pyramid on the horizon that was the nearest land was to the southwest.

He braced himself, then tried to relax as he hit the water. His life belt saved him and served him well, he stayed upright. He struggled to swim forward as he rose to the surface, and a moment later he saw the beautiful sun as he gasped for breath. His parachute was subsiding in a mass of billows, and he was not tangled in the lines. He was lucky. He had made it.

He unbuckled his parachute and started to swim westward.

The kit bobbed into view much sooner than he had expected, and quickly he inflated the life-raft and climbed aboard. Then he looked around for his fellow jumpers. He saw Tom and knew he was dead before he had even reached him. Blood colored the water, blood from a wound on his neck. Sick at heart, he unbuckled the parachute and hauled it on board, then removed the gun, personal kit and other things from the body, stowing them in the raft. Then he headed for the other swimmer.

The figure was struggling to free himself from the tangled parachute lines as he approached. He breathed a sigh of relief that this one was alive enough to move about in the water. At least he would not be alone. But as he saw who the man was, his breath caught in his throat. His heart began to pound at the recognition that this was his captain.

As he pulled him into the raft and collected the parachute, mental images of this same captain flashed through his mind— this captain with his almost white blond hair, eyebrows just as white, set in the rich copper of the tanned face—the square broad shoulders—the muscled arms with wrists twice as broad as his own—the trim hips in carefully tailored uniform pants— and always women, women forever surrounding him. Women made fools of themselves over this six-foot-four-inch Swedish type. Our corporal's thoughts were bitter.

He turned to look at the handsome face, and his heart skipped a beat as he saw the white eyebrows and the blond head of hair. The captain's eyes were closed. He moved over to the inert figure and started to remove the equipment and flying suit. Then he opened the first-aid kit and bandaged the gash in the upper arm. Even the touch of his muscled arm was a thrilling experience. The captain moaned and turned as the corporal gently propped up his head.

These wet clothes would have to come off, since they were completely water-soaked. He had removed his own in order to paddle easier. So he knelt by the unconscious figure and removed the shirt. He wondered if the captain had fainted from loss of blood or something else. He touched the smooth bronzed chest with the crisp white hairs glistening in the sun. He felt a stirring in his own loins. He ran his hand down the smooth flesh of the belt, then struggled with the pants until he had them off and spread out to dry.

The white jockey shorts were wet and almost transparent. They clung to their contents, outlining the organ and balls in clear, exciting relief. He ran his hand along the wet bulge, and felt the organ twitch. His spine tingled. He had wanted to do this, touch this magnificent basket since the first moment he had seen the captain. For a long moment, he sat looking at the beautiful sight, his fingers tracing the springy contents. Then the captain stirred, and the corporal sat back, waiting with bated breath, but the other man did not awaken, only sighed audibly.

"Those wet shorts must come off," he told himself, saying the words aloud. He put his hands into the white elastic band and began to work the shorts down over the slender hips. The man's flat muscled stomach seemed so defenseless in its whiteness. The contrast with the suntanned chest was very marked. A line of light brown hairs, almost but not quite blond, was like an arrow pointing toward the navel, the arrow lengthening and becoming dense as the shorts crept downward.

The cloth was at the root of the organ. The soft brown hair spread and curled thickly around the beautiful big pubes. He caught his breath as more and more of the organ came into view. It was broad and thick. "What a tool!" he thought. The end finally came into view, and he saw that it was uncircumcised, but a good quarter of the red glans was exposed. He touched it, drawing the foreskin back, exposing the whole glans to his gaze, holding the warm skin backward. He forced himself to turn away from the beautiful sight and to remove the shorts by drawing them down the long, well-muscled and tanned legs. His own organ was stiff and throbbing. He grasped it in his hand, but went no further. He opened some rations, and after eating and drinking, he lay down and went to sleep.

It was late in the afternoon when he awoke. He sat up and looked around. With relief he noted from the blue outline in the southwest that they had drifted closer to land. The captain was still asleep. The raft was dry and warm. Naked as he was, he was quite comfortable.

Then the captain stirred. The corporal knelt beside him and held some water to his lips. The captain drank, and then seemed to struggle to come to full consciousness. The corporal reached over to get some rations, and when he turned back he saw the captain was staring unbelievingly at the bare loins so close to his face.

"Corporal," the captain said faintly.

"Yes, captain," he answered, as he sat down to hide the erection he was afraid might develop. The captain did not say any more.

"Here, captain, eat something. You lost some blood," continued the corporal, placing a portion of rations in his hand. The captain ate a bit.

"How many made it?"he asked.

"Just two of us."

The captain sighed and closed his eyes, as his hand grasped the hand of the corporal holding the cup, and held it tightly. Then he seemed to drift off into sleep.

The moon was rising when the captain stirred again. He sat up and looked about. They ate and drank again, and then the corporal opened one of the little packs of cigarettes.

"Throw your shirt over you while you light them," cautioned the captain, "so the light won't show." The corporal did as he was told and handed a cigarette to the captain, who again cautioned him to cup the lighted cigarette in his hand so the glow would not show.

"Now bring me up-to-date on what happened," he said, after they had finished the cigarettes and were lying side by side. "Seems we are drifting towards that island. I'm sure we're much nearer than we were this afternoon."

The captain took advantage of the moonlight to survey his corporal: the black, short-cropped hair, down his pleasant, open face with the full, warm lips, onto his well-shaped chest with more dark hair, on down into the skin that wasn't tanned, lingering on the long, slender organ and smooth, round balls, but finally continuing along the lean, tanned legs. Then he began to talk, speculating on where they were, what had happened, and what was in store for them. He then tore the cigarette to pieces, crumpling the paper before he threw it away.

As he continued to talk, his hand ran lightly along the corporal's thigh. "How long do you think it will take us to drift to that island?" he asked, looking off to the horizon.

"I don't know," the corporal answered with difficulty, his heart pounding furiously at the captain's touch. "Three days, maybe," he was finally able to offer.

"Three days!" exclaimed the captain. "And then it might be days before we get picked up," he added, lying with his long, brown legs touching the corporal's. "And I have a date tonight with a little dream of a nurse." He moved restlessly. "And boy, does she know how to fuck! "

The corporal lay still, feeling the pressure of the warm hand on his thigh become heavier. He knew he would reveal himself any minute now by the action of his throbbing cock. He looked at the captain's crotch. He saw the beautiful love weapon slowly and jerkily begin to stiffen, as the captain muttered huskily, "God, it might be a week before we get back—a whole week without a cunt, and me with hot nuts right now." His cock was standing up straight and throbbing, its red head protruding from the foreskin which had been pulled back by the fullness of the erection.

The corporal could control his own cock no longer. It stood forth in its glory—lesser than the captain's, but in no way a minor spectacle.

"How about the babe you have waiting for you?" asked the captain. "I'll bet she has hot pants for you right now, too." The corporal's cock began to throb with excitement.

"You don't have to say a word, corporal. Your dong is answering for you." The captain looked at the erect seven inches of live meat, and rubbed his own cock with a long sigh that ended in a groan. "And look at that moon going to waste," he said. "Well, hot rocks or not, I guess all we can do is go to sleep and maybe have a wet dream," and he turned on his side and curled up.

The corporal lay still, his cock pounding. *God, it might be a week before we get back,* he thought, repeating the captain's lament. But his thought continued with, *A whole week lying next to that magnificent naked body with that great, throbbing joy stick so near.* And now those solid, round cheeks of that beautiful ass smiling at him. But he turned on his side, too, away from the captain, and soon he was in the world of wet dreams.

* * * * * * *

The next day was uneventful. They found paddles in the raft's kit, and spent much time rowing toward the island. Although their clothes were dry, the captain made no move to put on even his jockey shorts. The corporal remarked that they might get the untanned parts burned, and the captain joked. "Yes, we've got to be careful not to get our little pricks sunburned because we'll be wanting to put them to hard work when we get picked up."

The corporal found the sunburn lotion in the kit, and as they applied it, the captain said, "Say, this is slippery enough to lubricate a hot cunt." They both began to get hard-ons; the captain at his own thoughts, and the corporal when he saw once again the object of his desire. But they went back to their rowing. A rain squall came up, but they had covered everything with one of the parachutes, so no harm was done, and the coolness was pleasant.

That night the moon rose big and coppery. The captain went to sleep first, and the corporal lay for a time listening to his even, quiet breathing. Then he moved over close against the sleeping beauty, snuggled up so that his body fit the captains, and went happily to sleep.

The corporal woke up to find the moon brighter, but low in the sky. He had been sleeping for some time. Then he became aware of an unusual rhythmic motion beside him.

"What's going on?" he asked, still half asleep. But as he sat up and looked around, it became clear what was going on. The captain had moved back against the side of the raft, his legs spread wide, one on either side of the corporal, and his right hand was around his huge, pulsing cock. Startled by the corporal's waking, he grabbed a corner of the parachute and tried to cover his stiff staff. But the cloth continued to pulsate, and the corporal realized he had interrupted the captain just on the verge of coming.

The captain lay still for a moment, panting with his excitement, but obviously embarrassed. Then he sheepishly put his hand beneath the silk and began to stroke again.

"Oh God!" he said. "Why didn't you stay asleep one minute longer?" His motions became more excited, and he finally threw back the silk covering and the corporal gasped as the huge red head of the cock seemed to glow in the moonlight as the captain kept up his frantic motions. "What the hell! I can't stop now. I've fucked a cunt every night of my life, almost, since I was fourteen. Most times I've shot my load two or three times each night. Sometimes with the same gal, sometimes with a different one each time. It's damned uncomfortable having your cock and balls overflowing with cream and not be able to do anything about it." As he continued stroking, he looked at the corporal. "Well, Corporal, it looks like you're in just about the same fix I am!" and he laughed kindly.

The corporal's rod had risen to its full, throbbing proportions as he watched this beautiful blond man whose strong, tanned legs were rubbing against his own body now. He was almost in a state of shock. The excitement of watching the captain's excitement was driving him beside himself with desire.

The captain moved slightly so that he lay almost flat, his cock like a ship's mast. He reached over with his free hand and grasped the corporal's throbbing organ. "Ever have another man play with it before? When we were on bivouac and I couldn't get pussy, I found that my buddy was a damned good cocksucker.

He had a technique that was out of this world. Gee! Do I wish he were here now." The captain rubbed the corporal's prick slowly, up and down, up and down, the corporal was almost out of his mind as the pleasure mounted. The sensation of those strong brown fingers around his meat was almost too much for him.

Suddenly he moaned, leaned his head back, his legs thrown wide apart. His prick stiffened in the captain's warm grasp, and his body was convulsed as he moved to fuck the captain's hand. The captain's eyes glistened as he watched the gigantic spurts of white come. Several went clear over his head; one landed on his shoulder, and then as the subsiding cock reduced its power, gob after gob landed on the corporal's shaking body.

This was all the captain needed. His own body stiffened. "I'm coming! I-I-m-m-m coming!" He moaned, and as the corporal weakly turned his head, he saw the gism spurt from the huge cock and land on the brown chest and lighter belly.

They lay still, silent except for their still excited breathing. The corporal felt he should say something, but he couldn't make the effort. With a relaxed sigh, the captain released both cocks and put his hands over the side to wash away the come that had drooled down these well-spent organs. Then he sponged away the come from both their bodies, and wiped them dry with a bit of parachute.

"It's been a long time since I've jacked off," said the captain, "but damnit, we both needed it. I counted thirteen spurts of cream from you. You know, you're quite a man!"

"You say I'm a man!" exclaimed the corporal. "I wish I had a tool like yours. The girls must go crazy when they feel that ram-rod shoving its way up their twats." He leaned forward and lifted the captain's now limp but still sizeable prick. "I was dreaming of fucking when I woke up and saw you jacking off. I guess I thought it was still part of my dream. Maybe it is!" He played with the organ, running his fingers over the smooth glans, feeling the wetness at the end as a remaining drop of come oozed out.

"You do all right," the captain assured him, feeling the thrill of the corporal's hand on his sensitive tool. He looked at the other's crotch. "Boy, oh boy! You're still stiff!" He touched the corporal's now rigid organ. "Don't you ever go down?" The captain's cock was swelling again in the corporal's hand.

"I like sex," the corporal said simply. "Give me a hot cunt— or anything else that's hot and smooth—but just let me feel warm flesh around my cock." Both weapons were primed and ready for action again.

"Did you ever suck a cock?" asked the captain.

"When I'm hot enough I'll do anything," said the corporal, tightening his grasp on the captain's throbbing organ.

The captain's eyes glittered. He jerked the corporal's meat. "Suck me now," he pleaded, his breathing fast, his voice husky, his body already trembling in anticipation.

"I'm not that hot—yet!" the corporal replied.

The captain reached into the kit and got the container of suntan lotion. Digging his fingers into the cream, he smeared it on the corporal's cock. "This will make it feel juicy, like my hand is a hot cunt," he said, laughing, as he began stroking the slippery cock. The sensation was terrific.

The corporal moved so he could lean over and reach the captain's beautiful, vibrant meat with his lips. He just barely touched the tip of it at first, feeling the wetness of the head on his mouth. Now he knew he couldn't stop. He opened his lips and let the eager head in. He caressed it with his tongue, and the captain thrust his body up so that the entire ten inches went into the corporal's mouth. At last his nose was nestled in those beautiful hairs, and the masculine scent was a perfume to him, sending his senses reeling.

"Oh, baby!" moaned the captain. "Why did you let me waste that load jacking off!" He passionately ran his fingers through the corporal's black, crisp hair. His hips began rolling with the rhythmic sucking his cock was getting. He reached over and took the corporal's cock in his hand again and began jerking it.

The corporal stopped his work on the captain and sat up. "Not the hand, now, captain. Junior likes to slide into a warm mouth, too!" He moved so his cock was right by the captain's lips.

The captain turned his face away. "No, no! I can't do it," he said thickly.

"Come on, suck it!" the corporal grated through his teeth, and pushed against the captain's face. "It hasn't hurt me none."

The captain's blond head fell backward, and an expression of horror was on his face. "I just can't," he gasped.

The corporal grabbed him by the hair and pulled his head forward. "Open your mouth and take this cock." He shoved it against the captain's mouth and it went in. The captain retched miserably. The corporal moved back and looked at the shaken man, as saliva dripped from his still pulsing cock. But he noticed that the captain had totally lost his erection.

"I am sorry," the captain almost sobbed, "but I can't do it."

The corporal began to toy with his own cock, and then put the captain's limp one in his own hand. It didn't stay limp long. The corporal began jerking them rapidly. As the captain's passion rose again, he put his hand on the dark head and pushed it close to his booming cock.

"Suck it. Suck it!" he cried. "I'm hot as a firecracker...I'm almost ready to come.... Oh, suck it, baby!"

The corporal stopped his work again and sat up straight.

"I suck cock on a 50-50 basis only. You don't suck, I don't suck."

But he took the captain's demanding cock in his hand again and squeezed it hard as he brought his hand up to the protruding head, causing a large drop of pre-come to ooze out and drool down into his hand.

"Don't stop, don't stop now! Please!" begged the writhing captain. "I'll come in a minute now," and he made fast fucking motions into the corporal's hand.

Suddenly the corporal stopped rubbing the man's cock and ran his hand down over the balls and into the cheeks of his ass, massaging the tight little hole with his fingers. The captain gasped and spread his legs farther apart. The corporal bent down and took the sac of balls into his mouth, played with them a moment, and then bent the captain's legs upward so his tongue could travel along the ridge from the balls to the asshole, then around it.

"Oh, my corporal, my baby!" moaned the captain in ecstasy. "Oh, God! you're out of this world. Oh suck it, baby! Suck it!"

While he was doing this, the corporal reached into the suntan container and smeared the lotion on his own rod, and into the crack of the captain's ass, finally finger-fucking him deep. "Anybody ever been up there with a cock, Captain?"

"No, but if you don't stop that I'll blow my load."

The corporal bent so that he had one of the captain's legs on each of his shoulders, and steered his seven throbbing inches into the well-lubricated hole. The captain let out a cry of pain, and the corporal stopped.

"Relax, man," he said, as he lay still for a minute. "The pain will go away in a minute and you'll like my cock as much as you did my finger." Then he started the penetration again, slowly and very gently, playing with the captain's upstanding tit-points.

"You're right," the blond breathed happily in a moment. "It feels wonderful." Then the corporal shoved again—and again, until finally, when the probe had hit bottom, the captain winced but grinned up at the corporal. "Ouch! But don't stop now! I love it!"

The corporal bent over and, without too much effort, was able to take the entire head of the captain's roaring rod into his mouth, sucking gently as he fucked him wildly. All the way in until his balls slapped the captain's ass, then all the way out until just the head was still in the warm, smooth, clean asshole of the beautiful blond man. In and out, in and out, until the corporal knew by the electric shock that was rising up his spine that it wouldn't be long now. He was sucking more and more frantically as he fucked more violently. He heard the captain cry out with a great groan as his cock gave a great throb, and the corporal's mouth was filled with great spurts of sweet, rich cream. At this moment his own passion reached the peak and he exploded with all his love force into the writhing ass of his captain.

They fell together, breathing as runners who had completed the marathon. Then the corporal, after they had rested awhile, raised himself on his elbows and looked at the beautiful body and face beneath him.

The moonlight fell on his blond hair, the bronze skin, as the well-shaped nose twitched and the full, warm mouth smiled broadly up at him, showing white, even teeth gleaming in the silver light. A surge of feeling mixed with passion, possession, longing, fulfillment, and consuming love brought tears to the corporal's eyes, and he bent down and covered his captain's lips with a long passionate, tongue-searching kiss. The captain responded with equal ardor, showing no change when he realized he was tasting his own come. A great change was occurring which neither of them realized. They lay for a long time like this, with no words needed between them.

But finally the captain moaned gently, and said, "My ass hurts. What do you have up there?"

"Just my cock," laughed the corporal.

"God, I never felt anything like that before," almost purred the captain. "I think I could get used to it without any trouble."

"Let's rest now," the corporal suggested, knowing the captain would enjoy it even more when the soreness of the first entry cleared away. He pulled his hardening cock gently out of the relaxed ass, rolled the captain on his side, reached down and kissed both cheeks of his ass, then snuggled against him with his own hard cock pressed against the captain's back and his hand enclosing the warm love wand in front. Their organs soon subsided as they floated off into satisfied slumber.

But the corporal never seemed to be completely oblivious of the smooth flesh so close against his own. He awoke and raised his head. The moon was low in the sky, and the light flowed over the beautiful body in his arms. Gently, he ran his fingers along the throat muscles to the pit of the neck, then felt the firm, strong pectorals, feeling their springiness under his searching fingers, then searched until he found the paps. As he toyed with them, his cock became stiff and he pressed it into the firm buttocks in front of him. He ran his hand along the body, almost shivering with delight as he felt the sensation of the small blond hairs that covered the arms. He moved his hand to the navel and traced the sculptured effect of the muscled stomach. Feeling the short bristles just below the navel brought a surge of passion over him, his stiff prick throbbing in the captain's ass-cheeks.

He followed the line of hairs as they broadened into the pubes, matted now with moisture and semen of their passion together. He touched the soft cylinder of flesh lightly, and lifted it. He ran his finger over the end and felt the coolness of a drop of semen that was oozing from it. He ran his fingers down the solid, well-shaped leg, and then up the other one to the crotch. The scrotum was a delight, two lovely toys to be played with. Then his finger followed the ridge of flesh from the sac to the ass-hole, the short hairs tickling him like electric impulses. A bit of warm semen touched his fingers as he penetrated the anus of the beautiful blond god he was worshipping.

He returned to the soft cock. He drew back the foreskin and caressed the ridge of the glans. He touched his lips to the nape of the neck, as the smell and taste of the golden body intoxicated him beyond control.

He moved around so he was kneeling before the still sleeping captain. He leaned over, gently kissing the lips, the paps, the navel: his tongue followed the golden arrow down to the bush, where the tired warrior was lying limp. The captain breathed deeply and moved so that he was lying flat on his back: his cock swelled a little as though he was having a sensuous dream.

The corporal's cock was pounding. As he knelt before the man, drinking in his blond beauty, he grabbed his own cock in a fury of passion. Without jerking it at all, he began to have an orgasm as he shuddered ecstatically; great spurts of come jettisoned from his cock and fell like a libation on the golden body. Semen landed on the forehead, the throat, on the stomach, and as the force abated, the still swelling cock of the sleeping man was anointed. The captain, still asleep, moaned as though in a passionate embrace himself. The corporal, sobbing in the fullness of his emotion, stretched himself on top of his love, feeling the wetness of his own semen between them, yet uniting them. He dozed.

He awoke to find the bronze legs locked around his body, a stiff cock grinding into his navel. He looked into the blue eyes of the captain, now dark with passion, and in a flash his own penis was erect again. He raised his body, and the captain grabbed the two toys and began playing with them. Then he guided the one rising out of the crisp, black hair towards his own eager asshole.

The corporal felt the captain's body engulf his ready organ, and passion darted through him like lightening. He raised his buttocks and plunged his cock deeper, and the captain groaned, but with pleasure. Then he began to fuck at a merciless rate. But the captain met every thrust. The corporal bent to take the long, throbbing shaft that was so temptingly in reach, and the captain grabbed his head with loving fury and cried, "Suck it, lover, suck it!"

But soon the corporal became engrossed in his fucking. He arched his body, poised on the stiff ramrod that was entering the unresisting gales of the waiting ass, then sent the rod to its full depths in the warm softness beneath him. Again and again the happy citadel was attacked, faster and faster, until suddenly the corporal began to shudder as the loaded ramrod exploded, and once again the almost virgin ass was bathed with the hot gushing love juice.

"Suck my cock, baby!" gasped the captain. "I'm coming. I'm coming!" But the corporal was too excited to do anything but let his passion spend itself in great gasping jerks, so the captain grabbed his own throbbing rod and jerked furiously as his load shot forward, striking the corporal full in the face and drenched his chest and belly. As it ran down over his lips, his tongue caught it, tasting the wonderful richness of the vitality of the man. Then they fell together again and lay still for a long time, finally rolling on their sides, still glued together by the captain's spend.

The corporal awoke to the sensation of someone playing with his half-hard cock. At the same moment, he realized who it was, and his prick came to full attention. He opened his eyes to see the captain straddling him, his ass poised over the thrusting prick. He felt the smoothness of the suntan lotion as the captain massaged the weapon, so engrossed in his work that he didn't know he was awake. The corporal watched as the golden-bodied man lowered himself onto the now fully extended prick which slipped into the stretched opening with ease, sending a glow of excitement through the groin and belly of the reclining corporal. The captain pulled the muscles of his ass, and the corporal felt the tightness draw about his raging organ. His excitement rose as he watched the buttocks raise and lower on his tool, most of it visible to him at the peak of the motion. The captain's own formidable cock was flapping about before his face, raising his passion once again to the boiling point. Feeling the throbs of the corporal's approaching orgasm, the captain sank to the hilt, closed his eyes, and reveled in the flow of sperm deep within him.

The tantalizing temptation of the turgid tool before him was too much for the thrilled corporal, and he raised his body so he could sink it deep in his eager mouth. The captain moaned with pleasure and grasped the dark head, holding it down on his throbbing pole until it was gushing forth a flood of life fluid.

The day passed uneventfully, except for sporadic rowing toward the island which neither one was really very eager about reaching, except they realized the rations could not last forever, and the sun sometimes did get rather annoying, even with what suntan lotion they could spare from their more exciting use of it.

That night, after they had slept for some time, the captain was lying sprawled on his back, wondering if they would ever be picked up. Then he looked up at his corporal leaning over him, and all worry thoughts fled. Raising his arms and circling the hard, young body, passion glowed in his blue eyes as he gazed into the handsome face of his corporal. Realizing the message in those eyes, the corporal, without further delay, swung around into a sixty-nine position, still arched over the captain, and thrust his hot cock into the eager, open lips beneath him. The captain clasped him about his slim buttocks and drew him passionately close to him. His hands reached through the corporal's muscled thighs and lovingly caressed his balls, sucking avidly on the thrusting cock. There was no horror now, no gagging, only the hope that this would never end, and yet wanting that first wonderful sensation of come spurting into his mouth. This change that had been unconsciously wrought in him several nights ago when he tasted his own come on the corporal's kiss was now being manifest.

The corporal was beside himself with excitement. He grasped the blond head, roughly—the roughness of loving passion— guiding it in its motions on his cock, running his fingers through the soft hair. His thighs quivered with each caress of his well filled sac, and the captain's body rose and fell as he became more entranced by his sucking of the corporal.

"Don't make me come yet!" gasped the corporal, pulling his cock from the reaching mouth, which immediately began tonguing his balls, his hands still playing with the corporal's buttocks and ass.

The corporal moved down so he, too, was taking the captain's balls in his mouth. Then his lips went exploring the path to that cave that had given him so much pleasure these past days. His tongue found it, and darted in as the corporal spread the beautiful cheeks for better access. He probed and sucked as he reached around and grasped the throbbing cock that was pushing into his chest.

He pulled himself back into position so he could take the pushing member into his mouth, and the captain, in eager ecstasy, pushed that huge hunk of meat to the hilt into the corporal's open throat, at the same time renewing his newly acquired art of sucking on the corporal's now drooling penis. Both wanted this to last forever, but also wanted it to end in an immediate explosion—and that is what happened. In the simultaneity of passionate love, they released together, drinking and serving each other in pure perfection. It was a moonless night with stars crowding each other in the vast heavens as fireworks exploded in the heaven of two lost, floating soldiers who had never been happier....

* * * * * * *

The next day they were picked up by a troop ship, and as they were helped aboard, they could see the white beach of the island they almost reached. What would have happened had they reached that island??? On board the ship was civilization—and nurses. Immediately, the captain was excited with the habitual prospects before him. The corporal, remembering the golden body which was his to fondle, to nuzzle, kiss, to fuck and suck for the past eternity of three days, was a sad G.I. But they were received as heroes. The captain reveled in the attention, kissing every pretty nurse in reach; the corporal remained quiet, only speaking to answer questions about the wrecked plane. Of course, the ship was crowded, and the captain apologized about shortage of space for the new arrivals. The captain insisted that the corporal share his cabin. The corporal's spirits rose.

Soon, however, they were dampened when the captain, in the cabin, turned to the corporal and said, "Glad to have you in the cabin, corporal. I know you'll be scarce when I get some of these cute little cunts in here for a little work-out, won't you? You can do the same, if you'll give me the word." The corporal's bubble burst.

Dinner was dominated by the captain, his handsome face and even slimmer figure, the cynosure of all eyes. The corporal was given some attention, but it left him unimpressed. He excused himself early, saying he was very tired, and went to bed. He pulled the curtain that separated the two bunks, and although the bed was wonderfully soft after the raft, he would have given anything to be back there with his lost idol. The sound of the party on deck was in his ears as he went to sleep. He didn't sleep well.

The noise of the opening of the cabin door wakened him. A little moonlight splashed through the porthole. He heard the sound of clothes being removed, and his heart sank. He dreaded the thought of having to listen to the sounds of sex that would be forthcoming shortly. He turned to the wall and put the pillow over his ears.

Someone was sliding the curtain back. He felt his bed move as someone slid in. Strong arms went around him. A long body touched him from head to foot. Unbelieving, he turned and warm, avid lips sought his.

"I love you," said the captain, as his tongue returned to the lips of his choice.

PART THREE
A TOUCH OF CLASS

The following stories share rather a unique common denominator—unique among Tijuana Bible stories, that is; both of them achieve a state of literary quality not usually found in this material.

That is not to say that either *George* or *One August Afternoon* stands at a prize-winning level. But they do outshine most such material, and are probably considerably better than a lot of what is foisted on the reading public of today as "literature".

The first of the two, *One August Afternoon,* is probably the better of the two, and the more unique. Unique if only in that the "action" doesn't start for quite a while—not until almost the second third. And in that first segment, the author (unknown, as they always are in these things) attempts what is rarely attempted in these stories. He establishes characterization, he develops a plot, sketches background and mood—in short, he attempts to make an honest story out of this little adventure.

His success is not complete. Some of the characters blur—most of those presented in the beginning, in fact, have nothing to do with the story. The plot, thin at best, relies for the most part on coincidence and hyperbole. The background remains vaguely seen, and the mood ultimately resorts to the usual rampant sexuality.

But Mother Ash and Lana are real people, familiar to the habituees of the gay world. More surprisingly so are the boys whom our hero encounters. Surprising, because it is here that most such writers falter, yielding to an all too obvious fantasy—letting every male, however straight and innocent, be converted in one lick to a devout homosexual. But not so our young men. Joe is a young hedonist, but he remains essentially an oversexed but heterosexual young man. Tony resorts to the excitement of voyeurism, but his resentment and anger are convincing. Tree climbing Eddie remains youthfully unspoiled.

And if Hal succumbs to the erotic cliches of such material, he does so with due deference to his companions, and resists the author's urge to have him look back and wave when it is done. As for our hero, who is not the best characterization, we are at least gratified to find that he is finally "so bored and tired of that miserable cock!" In another story, he would have been thrilled again...and again...and again, sometimes ad nauseam.

George falls considerably short of this high mark. The plot is nothing more than the usual excuses for getting sex started. For background, we know that some scenes occur around a college and others on an island beach, but there are no details of description to distract us from the purpose. And the hero remains only a nebulous "I" with which few readers will be unable to identify.

But into George, the title character, the author has put more, and however flimsy the story he tells, he occasionally finds the artful phrase for telling it. When he tells you that meeting George is like "walking up to a hot stove after you have been half frozen with the cold," or..., "Like a tall, cold glass of water after sweltering in the desert all day," we get the point.

As to the flaws—well, our author does us the courtesy at least of a fair warning, as to what we should expect: "If you don't want to beat your meat, then stop right here. You can't possibly finish this tale with a dry cock." It would be unfair, after such an honest preamble, to expect a Dickens or Thackeray.

CHAPTER EIGHT
ONE AUGUST AFTERNOON

"More eggs, anyone?" Freddy Ash cried out cheerily as he bent his six foot four hulk over the campfire, happily splashing hot bacon grease around in a skillet full of eggs. The response was unanimous. Even I decided to have another—my fourth. The pan held only six eggs, so we each got one.

I looked up as Freddy plopped an egg into my plate. He could well afford to be more cheerful than the rest of us, I thought. Didn't we sit through all of breakfast while he regaled us with tales of his nocturnal adventures of the night before? Didn't he take the greatest delight in tormenting us with detailed descriptions of each and every one of his eight conquests? The five teen-age boys in sleeping bags down by the lakeshore—the two fishermen in a truck parked near-by—and, the "lovely" milkman who just happened to stop to pee as your tired old "Mother" stepped from the truck after doing those two magnificent numbers...and so on.

While the rest of us spent the whole evening tearing up the road between Inglenook and the Green Light, "Mother" Ash confined his activities to the dark shoreline, plucking juicy hors d'oeuvres from responsive sleepers or else melting into the night whenever encountering some uncooperative little devil who would have his head.

The rest of us were usually dead asleep by midnight. Mother Ash, at the same time, was just getting started. In the soft weak light of dawn, his tall, lean figure could be seen loping along the deserted road leading back to camp, swinging his flashlight at each and every fallen tree or stump or anything else that looked like it might be a human in distress! He constantly hoped for some unfortunate male that had had one too many and couldn't quite make it back to camp without a moment's rest. Ash was most thorough! He exhausted every possibility before giving up, reluctantly, for the night.

Invariably, upon his return, Mother would discover that some or all of his bedding had been snatched up by some thoughtless weekend guest.

On this particular weekend, the guest happened to be a little swish from the West Side—more popularly known in his own circle of friends as Lana. Lana entertained us royally on the drive up. She told one impossible tale after another and insisted on screaming at every passing car that contained a male! This screaming queen irked Mother Ash immensely. Ash, being strictly a trade queen, had little use for screaming faggots, and Lana was about the worst of them all!

Mother Ash adored cooking over an open fire. He planned the menu and supervised all the shopping for the entire weekend. Came that wonderful hour just before dinnertime, when the sun ducked behind the high hill to the west, Ash would go about making all sorts of preparations and shooing my guests off into the woods for firewood.

"Now listen, you faggots," Ash warned as he lifted the skillet full of bacon fat from the fire. "Don't any of you kick dirt into this pan. Tonight your Mother is going to cook you the best fried chicken you ever ate! And—we'll have tons of corn— roasted right in the hot coals!" Ash was in surprisingly good form this morning despite very little sleep. He paused to let this good news sink in, "So don't any of you come back to camp tonight empty-handed. Bring some firewood with you—lots of it. And another thing—I'm warning all of you to stay away from that camp at the head of the lake. That territory is exclusively for your Mother. I've spent all summer working on those boys and I don't want any of you bitches cutting in on my territory!"

Oh, this outdoor life made Freddy a jolly one! The camp he mentioned was inhabited by four young boys They had been camping there most of the summer and no one but Freddy had the guts to try to strike up a conversation with them. According to him, the boys always ran around completely nude! He watched them carry firewood, swing from trees and even gave a detailed account of one of them pissing. Ash spent many anxious hours crouched in the thick brush watching them and waiting for one to break away from the group— So far, they stuck pretty close together.

But Ash was not easily discouraged. It was only the first week of August, and a great deal could happen between now and Labor Day.

Mother was pouring more coffee. He filled the West Side Weasel's cup and was turning away when Lana spoke up.

"But my dear Mother Ash," wailed Lana, "I hardly think it was necessary to buy five whole fryers for only six people. After all, how much chicken can a girl eat? It isn't the money, you know."

"What!" cried Mother, an incredulous look coming over his rugged face, "What did you say?"

"I mean—we're not pigs, after all—and as for me—I usually nibble on a small piece of breast. That's all!"

"Don't we all," said another of my guests.

Freddy Ash, always eager to squeeze drama from any and all situations, glanced quickly at the two empty egg cartons, the bacon wrappings, the third pot of coffee, the fourth Dugan's coffee ring that was being devoured and then at me! I didn't know what to say, so I merely shrugged my shoulders. The gesture was enough for Freddy. He straightened up majestically to his full height and looked the hapless Lana straight in the eye.

"My darling," Mother bitched cuttingly. "Let's put it this way. When we break up camp tonight, I'll pack all the food that's left over, for you to take home—does that meet with your highnesses approval, my sweet?"

"I meant no offense," said the weasel.

"I know, darling," said Ash, "neither did I!"

Ash turned away from the weasel and busied himself with the fire, muttering derogatory remarks about the West Side and its "Screaming" inhabitants.

I was not disturbed. Past experience had taught us that one could never buy too much food for a weekend at the lake. We knew that before the night was out, the whole bunch of them would be gnawing the chicken bones and even cracking them to suck out the marrow.

Breakfast done with, Ash banked the fire and we all sat in front of the tent and looked out over the water. It was quite early, the sun was getting warmer and everyone was getting into their trunks.

The talk got around to sex—as usual. That's all my guests ever did—talk sex. Mother Ash had the floor. "Now this taxi driver was so gorgeous your mother just had to proposition him! Big—and so butch, too! He came up willingly enough—too willingly, as a matter of fact, and then makes a bee-line for my john and I'm sitting on my bed waiting and waiting and waiting! Mae! I could not stand the suspense another minute so I barged in on him. There she lay—stark naked in my bathtub without a drop of water in it. And do you know what she wanted your Mother to do?" Ash's eyes darted from face to face for someone to see him.

"What," cried Lana. "What?"

"Well, get this," continued Ash, "she wanted me to pee on her— Imagine!"

"Oh, no! How disgusting!" screamed the weasel, "—did you?"

"Of course not! I tried to do her but she just wouldn't let me."

"How absolutely maddening!" cried Lana.

"So...your mother threw her out and cruised up a real lovely number."

"Good for you," cried Lana. I could see where these two still might be great friends before the day was out.

I dashed into the tent and packed my little bag with cigarettes, soap and olive oil (which I used for tanning) and tossed in a carton of beer—just in case.

"That reminds me of the time—" the weasel was saying, as I dashed out of earshot and headed for the peace and quiet of the woods. I looked back and saw that Mother Ash wouldn't be around to hear about Lana's time, either. Ash was making fast tracks for the latrine, just a few yards behind a lovely number.

Following a trail that ran north along the lake, I came to the popular swimming hole called "Chair Rock." Being so early in the morning, the area was deserted. Later in the day, dozens of boys would take over, diving off the high rock or just sitting around getting tanned. It was a marvelous place for a queen to go out of her mind!

A couple of miles above "Chair Rock," a small brook tumbled into the main lake. Many alcoves dotted this area. Lovers beached their canoes at these points, and would go off into the thick woods to fuck, make love or just to be alone.

A couple of miles further up was the camp Ash warned us against visiting. I decided to look in on it just for kicks. There was nothing much to be seen; Aside from a small tent, a line was stretched between trees from which towels, swim suits and jock straps hung. To one side of the tent a hammock was strung and someone was lying in it. An extremely muscular leg hung outside of the hammock but I could see nothing of the person—just a leg. I looked for a long time and then walked back to the small brook and started to follow it back into the hills.

About a half mile up (it seems miles) there was a deep pool. The rocks here were flat and covered with smooth, thick moss. I called this my "Green Room"—my hideaway whenever I wanted to be alone. People rarely climbed to this point, so one could sunbathe in the nude without a single interruption.

The water being spring fed was ice cold. I put my cans of beer in the water and slipped out of my trunks. The sun felt warm and good on my naked body. I lit a cigarette and lay down on the cool moss. I closed my eyes and inhaled the smoke and listened to the water as it rushed over the rocks and on down to the lake. Now and then I heard the metallic booming of an aluminum canoe as lovers attempted to beach in a rocky cove. The faint sounds of people at the main beach could be heard far off....

The sun made me drowsy. Flicking my cigarette into the pool, I started covering myself with oil. I had a good tan except where my suit covered my body. On this tender, white skin, I poured the oil on thickly—massaging it well into my crotch, around my balls and ass and even under my foreskin—just in case I got a hard-on while asleep. The delicious combination of oil and massaging had its effect.

My hand was soon filled with my stiff, eight inch cock. I was damn close to shooting off, but decided to hold back until later. I fingered my balls slowly and tenderly as I dozed off to sleep.

About two hours later I was awakened by the sound of voices. Still half asleep, I wasn't sure just where the sound came from. It sounded rather close, but since no one ever climbed this far upstream, I thought—but no! There it was again, and much closer now!

I reached for my trunks and crawled to the edge of the pool and peered through the thick foliage to see if any girls might be making the climb. I saw two boys of about sixteen or seventeen. They were having a rough time of it. Then around a corner of a rock two other boys of the same age appeared. The first two stopped to wait for the others to catch up with them. They all wore trunks. Seeing no girls in the group, I tossed my trunks aside and lay down to wait....

The boys soon appeared above the rocks. They were very surprised to see me, and I feigned surprise upon seeing them. I waved and said "Hi," and asked them to join me.

I studied them closely as each one climbed down to where I stood. The first was a dark-haired, good-looking boy wearing a pair of surplus Navy trunks that revealed a huge bulge that was unmistakably his cock. The next was a blond with a short crew-cut. He was tall and wiry and wore skin-tight white satin trunks that stretched tightly over a healthy bulge—He didn't appeal to me at all. The third was dark and very Italian-looking. He was huge and seemed older than the others. He was a mass of muscles and his powerful legs were covered with fine, jet-black hair. He wore maroon boxer trunks that revealed nothing at all.

The last was a magnificent blonde. He wore a pair of cut-down dungarees and it was hard to tell if the bulge was the stitching on his fly or his cock. He looked very young. He had a Navy cap perched on his head and wore dirty white sneakers. His body was the most exciting I had ever seen!

"I'm Pete," I said by way of introduction. "Who are you guys?" I dropped my voice to sound as masculine as possible.

"I'm Joe," said the boy wearing the Navy trunks. "That's Eddie," he pointed to the thin blond..., "and his kid brother, Hal." He indicated the delicious-looking kid with the sailor cap. "And that dago bastard—he's Tony." Tony gave Joe a dirty look. They all said "Hi" except Tony. He seemed a little annoyed. Perhaps it was because I was standing there in the nude!

"Howdy," I said, and offered them cigarettes. We all sat down to smoke. Tony was definitely the oldest. They all had a fine growth of hair on their legs, but Tony was the only one with any hair on his chest. Hard as I tried, I couldn't keep my eyes off Hal. I had never seen a man so magnificently perfect. My eyes devoured every inch of his bare flesh.... I noticed Joe watching me closely. He was a smart cookie and had summed up the situation at once. I could tell from his attitude that he had me figured. He was giving me little, strange, knowing smiles and he kept adjusting his basket and watching my reaction. He had a half hard-on and made no attempt to hide it. In fact—he was obviously flaunting it in my face! Once when I looked up from his basket, he winked at me. I was quivering with excitement and a little nervous. Nevertheless, I knew then and there—nerves or no nerves—if I could get these boys separated, Joe would be a dead duck!

Tony finished his cigarette and stood up. "Let's get going," he said, "It's getting hot here." I wondered how he meant that. He seemed keenly aware of the little play that was going on between Joe and me.

Hal and Eddie jumped to their feet, but Joe didn't move. He told Tony he was too tired to do any more "exploring", and would meet them back here. I felt a growing excitement upon hearing this! I had a violent urge to do a little "exploring" myself, and Joe was my target. My pulse beat fast as I watched the boys disappear into the woods above us.

I turned back to Joe. He was stretched out on his belly watching me. He had kicked off his moccasins and was smoking another of my cigarettes. My eyes ran over his powerful body and stopped on his firm, round ass.... His tight swim suit was caught deep in the crack! As I stared, he started to move his ass slowly up and down. I walked over and sat down in front of him.

"How old is Tony?" I asked. I could have kicked myself for showing an interest in anyone but my immediate prey.

"He's eighteen," said Joe.

"He's a big guy," I remarked.

"Yeah," he replied. "Ya like 'em big?"

"You bet!" I said. I wondered if he meant the same thing I did. There was little doubt. This Joe was quick at grasping a situation.

"Me and Eddie is seventeen and Hallie is only fifteen," he said. He swung his body around bringing his crotch directly in front of me. His legs were spread out as far as possible. He had a roaring hard-on that all but pushed itself through the thin material! As I stared, Joe pushed himself to his feet and stood in front of me—his huge bulge only inches from my mouth!

"Gotta take a leak," he said. He strode over to the pool and stepped into ankle-deep water. Then he undid the drawstring on his suit and pulled it down just below his beautifully rounded ass. He stood there, his back to me—his hands lightly resting on his lean hips. I waited impatiently for the sound of piss, but it didn't come. Unable to bear the suspense any longer, I got to my feet and walked over to where he stood. I had to take a firm grip on myself when I saw his cock. It pushed out in front of him a good eight inches and its sharp, pointed head was throbbing wildly! I knew damn well that Joe didn't have to piss any more than I did!

"What in hell you *got* there?" he answered, taking the stiff thing into his hand and pointing it at me. "I *always* get a hard-on when I'm in the woods like this."

"That's a hell of lot of cock for a kid," I said.

"Hell, mister, I'm no kid," he shouted indignantly. "I'm seventeen and I fuck girls all the time!"

He stepped out of his trunks and threw them aside. Taking his cock in both hands, he waved it up and down at me, shouting—"DOES THAT LOOK LIKE A KID'S COCK? DOES IT?"

"Hell, no," I apologized. "That's a man's cock if I ever saw one!" I dropped to one knee for a close look.

"Ya damn right it is," he said, letting the huge thing fall between his legs.

"Man! It sure is a beauty!" I gasped, finding it difficult to keep my voice steady. My own cock stuck out in front of me like an old yard stick!

"It's big, huh?" he asked. "Ya like 'em big."

"It's the biggest cock I ever saw," I lied. But...it was bigger than most.

"I gotta do something about this," he said, walking over and spreading himself out on my towel.

"What do you do when you get a hard-on in the woods like this, Joe" I asked eagerly, as I joined him on the towel.

"This," he said, spreading his legs and taking his cock in his hand. He gave it about two strokes and I sprang into action!

"Like hell you do!" I cried, pushing his hand aside. "Not with me around you don't!"

I hardly had the head in my mouth when Joe started rubbing my head and pushing against my face. Before I even got the whole cock wet, he shot off into my mouth. I swallowed furiously as the hot tasty come squirted against the roof of my mouth. I was bitterly disappointed at the small amount he shot.

"Boy," I said, "that sure tasted great, Joe!"

"Christ, don't stop now, Pete!" he cried, pushing my head

down on it again. "I ain't finished yet!"

This time I had a chance to take it all. It was so hard that I had difficulty getting it all the way down my throat. I gave it a few licks and Joe was off again. He shot off about as much come as the first time.

"Well, I guess that finishes you off, eh, Joe?"

"Oh, no it don't," he said. "Give me a minute and I'll be ready for another time."

"How about a swim, meanwhile?" I asked.

"I'm with ya," he said, and ran toward the pool. I dove into the icy water after him and we swam around for a while and then crawled back into the hot sun to dry. Joe lit another of my cigarettes and lay down on his back to enjoy it. I fingered his big balls and watched as his soft cock grew hard under my touch! I pushed my face into his crotch and began to lick his balls. Joe was going out of his mind! I looked up to watch his cock throb when I was startled to see Eddie, Hal and Tony emerge suddenly from around a rock.

"Your friends have come back, Joe!" I whispered nervously.

"To hell with them!" he said, pushing my face down on his balls again. It was too late anyway. They had seen us

"Boy!" cried Eddie. "What's going on here?"

"Shut-up!" moaned Joe.

Tony didn't seem surprised at all, and merely walked over to a shady spot and sat down. Hal lay down on a rock about ten feet away and didn't bother to watch Joe and me.

Eddie was enjoying the whole thing. He sat close by and watched every move I made. After a moment, I stopped working on Joe's balls and took his cock into my mouth. I soon had him off for the third time!

I sat up and lit a cigarette. Eddie kept saying "Boy!" till I wanted to kick him. He all but applauded when Joe came off! I looked at Tony and he looked back at me with great disgust.

"Fuckin' fruit!" Tony said—more to himself than anyone else. "They're everyplace!"

"Shut up!"said Joe. "Who's bothering you?"

"For Christ sakes, you guys, let's get the hell out of here," said Tony. "I'm dying for a drink of water."

"Drink from the stream," I suggested.

"You nuts?" he said.

"Hell, no," I replied with a shrug. "I drink that water all the time. It's good."

"You suck cock, too, mister!" he sneered, "and don't try to tell me that's good!"

"So...?" I shrugged.

"So don't expect other people to do what you do, and don't get so goddamn smart with me if you know what's good for you, see, wise guy?"

I know this would only lead to trouble, and since I was outnumbered four to one, I decided it would be smarter to shut up. At that moment I hated Tony!

From where I sat, I could see his feet and part of his legs without making it obvious that I was looking. But, despite all my efforts, I couldn't help but follow the line of enormous muscles that ran from his calf to his crotch, and I soon found myself staring hard at his basket. The more I stared, the more I realized how desperately I wanted him!

His maroon trunks were pulled to one side and I could see a lot of hair, but nothing more than the bulge of one of his balls pushing against his jock.

Then I remembered my beer! It should be ice cold by now. I walked over to the pool and fished out five cans. I offered the first to Tony. He looked up at me rather kindly, and for the first time, I felt that things between us might warm up a little...!

Eddie and Joe opened their cans and I opened one for Hal. I walked over to where Hal lay but he made no move. Tony had gulped his beer in one swig and was more than eager to drink Hal's, so I gave it to him. We sat around drinking my beer and smoking my cigarettes.

"Ya like to suck cock, Pete?" Eddie asked. Joe answered for me. "Bet your ass he does. I never had a job like he gives! Makes Nancy stink!"

"Thanks, Joe," I said smiling. I was so relieved to have the party in a good mood again.

"Nancy stinks...even after a bath," laughed Eddie.

"Who in hell is this Nancy?" I asked. My curiosity had the better of me.

"Some whore we guys know," said Eddie. "Hey Joe, get it up! I wanna watch Pete suck you off!"

"Gimme a minute. Gimme a minute," Joe said. "I shot off three times already! What you think I am?"

"Three times? Huh!" said Eddie, disgustedly. "Three times is nothin' for you, Joe. Who ya kidding? Ya jerk off five or six times a day—don't ya?"

"Yeah," said Joe. "But that's in a day. I only been here an hour already."

I could see they were getting a little high, and decided to get more beer for them. I walked over to the pool and as I was naked, and it was hot as hell, I decided to have a short swim. The water was wonderfully cold and I stayed in for a moment before digging up the beer.

As I walked back I noticed that Eddie was climbing a tree. Crazy bastard! Why is it that when some guys get a drink in them they get a yen to climb things? Ed perched himself on a limb and yelled down to me. "Hey Pete," he was laughing, "look what Joe's got for ya!"

Joe had a roaring hard-on and he was jerking it slowly and swinging it around. "For you, Pete," he said.

"I'll take care of that in a minute, Joe." But I didn't relish the thought of doing Joe again. His cock was too hard—like a piece of steel, and my poor jaws were sore from sucking on it.

"No rush, Pete," he said. "No rush. We got all day, eh?"

"Sure, Joe," I said. "Meanwhile, how's about a fresh beer?"

"Sure," said Joe. Then, "Hey, Pete. What about the monkey," he nodded his head in Eddie's direction. Ed was hanging from a branch, swinging back and forth.

"What about him?" I asked.

"Will you suck him off, Pete?" asked Joe. I looked at Eddie.

I couldn't get excited over those skinny legs or that lean torso. And that hideous satin swim suit made me ill.

"Will ya, Pete?" asked Eddie, eagerly. "Will ya?"

"What in hell do you want me to do?" I asked, "Climb the tree to get at you?"

"Why not?" said Joe. "It's your pleasure."

"Soon as I finish this," I said, waving my beer at him. Meanwhile, I looked over at Tony. He was still sitting on the rock with his legs sprawled apart. He held his third beer in one hand while the other rested on his hairy, muscular thigh. My heart stopped when I saw that one of his balls had slipped from the jock and lay against his leg. It was almost buried in a thick mat of hair. I had the wildest desire to rip his trunks off and bury my face in his hairy crotch!

I finished my beer and walked over to Ed. What had I to lose? I've had a goodly share of stiff three-inch cocks pushed in my face before and one more could not kill me.

His crotch was on an even plane with my face. I was bored as I undid the drawstring and slipped his suit down. I damn near fell to my knees from shock! The little bastard, for all his skin and bone, had a cock that hung at least five inches! And it was limber!

"Jeez, you sure fooled the hell out of me, kid!" I cried, my heart throbbing wildly!

"That's nothin', Pete," said Joe, "Wait till you get it hard! They call Eddie 'big dick' at the Y."

I took the whole, soft cock into my mouth and began to run my tongue over it. I could feel it grow bigger and bigger and harder and harder. I waited till it was fully hard, then pulled it out of my mouth so I could look at it. It was one of those huge cocks that I could suck on all night and never tire! Thick, long and soft enough to slide down your throat with no trouble!

"Christ, don't just look at it!" cried Eddie, twisting his body toward me. "Take it...take it! "

Wild with passion, I took it all the way down my throat. I could feel the enormous head throbbing deep inside me.

Eddie was groaning and trying to fuck my face. With one great heave he lifted his legs up around my neck! His heels dug into my back and he was able to exert a lot more pressure in this position!

I held Eddie's ass in my hands and lifted it to help his every thrust! He let go of the branch and held on to my head. He pushed his cock deep into my mouth and said, "Christ, Pete. Where in hell does it all go? It feels just like it's sliding up a hot cunt! Boy!"

Naturally, I couldn't answer, but I was enormously flattered at what he said!

His ass moved faster and faster, his hard little buttocks closing tightly over my fingers with each frantic thrust. Before I realized what was happening, he rammed his cock full force down my throat and shot off a huge load! He eased back and shot more come in my mouth. It splashed against the back of my throat in huge gobs! IT WAS THICK AND CREAMY AND I GULPED IT DOWN EAGERLY!

He continued to fuck my face slowly and I could feel the magnificent cock getting soft.

I could feel his sweaty balls pushing against my chin and I wanted so much to suck on them!

I carried Ed to where Joe sat, drinking beer and enjoying our little "show". I squatted to let him hop off me. He sprawled out on his back next to Joe and I pushed my face into his crotch and took his sweaty balls in my mouth and sucked on them for a while.

"Ya like it, Eddie?"

"Damn right!" he said. "Better'n any cunt I ever fucked!"

"Ya see," said Joe, "I told ya. Pete puts 'love' or something in it when he sucks you off!"

"Ya ain't kiddin'," said Eddie, taking a long breath.

I lay back panting like a scared rabbit. I was eating up this delightful conversation when I felt someone straddle me and sit on my chest! Joe, I thought, cursing to myself! Damn that little punk! Why in hell doesn't he go off somewhere and leave me alone! I was too beat to face that lousy piece of meat again! Sure, an hour ago I would have given my right arm just to have a look at his cock, but I had it. I was sick and tired of Joe! I wished to hell he was anywhere but on my chest!

"Ah, Christ no!" I moaned aloud, hoping Joe would take the hint and leave me alone. "I've had all the cock I can handle for one day!"

"Oh no you ain't, mister!" said a voice that wasn't Joe's! A beer can crashed against a rock and fell in the pool with a splash! A hand lifted my head off the ground! I felt a cock—hard and hot being pushed against my closed lips! I reached for the legs that pressed against my sides and ran my hands up and down the hard, smooth, hairy muscles! TONY!

I opened my eyes and saw Tony's cock throbbing an inch from my mouth. It was as thick as Ed's but not quite as long. It was one of those magnificent, man-sized cocks that curves slightly downward. The dark skin that covered it was smooth and silky! It stretched tightly over the head and ended in an extremely long foreskin. A thick line of black hair ran from his cock up across his hard belly and stopped at his navel.

The intoxicating smell of Tony's sweating crotch filled me with a passionate yearning! I opened my mouth to take his cock, but Tony had other ideas.

He raised his ass over my face and placed his sweaty, HAIRY BALLS DIRECTLY OVER MY MOUTH! They were incredibly smooth as they brushed against my quivering lips.

"The works!" whispered Tony, his voice husky, menacing! "GIVE ME THE WORKS, YOU COCKSUCKER!" He was roaring drunk!

He began to move his ass slowly back and forth over my face. The crack of his ass brushed my lips and my hot tongue darted out and made contact with his hot flesh! My tongue ran madly through the crack seeking, searching, probing! When my tongue found its mark, Tony pressed his ass hard down on my face. He made a wild noise that sounded more animal than human as I continued licking and jabbing frantically at his asshole. After a few minutes of this, Tony started moving his ass around and around and stopping now and then to press down on my tongue whenever it happened to give him the most pleasure!

He finally had his fill of this and eased his body up a little, bringing his balls over my face again. I sucked them into my mouth and tongued them till I thought he would go mad! I bit off pieces of hair and swallowed them!

Tony suddenly pulled his balls out of my mouth. "SUCK ME OFF—NOW!" he cried passionately. "SUCK MY GODDAMNED COCK TILL I SHOOT OFF IN YOUR FACE!"

His cock lay throbbing against my trembling lips. I reached up and eased the long foreskin back, revealing a huge, red head. A wild cry broke from my lips as I lunged forward and took the head of Tony's cock in my mouth!

I was whimpering like a child as I sucked wildly on Tony's cock. Tony rammed it down my throat with a fierce, savage thrust!

I buried my nose in his thick pubic hair, inhaling the warm, sexy smell of his crotch!

"Jeez!" I heard Eddie say.

"Give it to him, Tony boy!" urged Joe.

"Give the bastard hell!"

"Boy!" cried Eddie. "Feels just like a cunt, eh, Tony!"

Tony was doing all right by himself! He needed no encouragement from those two punks!

Tony knew how to squeeze every ounce of joy from his sex! Never had I encountered a purer, more savage violence! I reached around and grabbed the cheeks of his ass. They were smooth and very hard. I dug my fingers deep into the hairy crack and held the muscular buttocks tightly in my hands.

Tony held my head in his hands and moved it up and down, matching the beautifully controlled action of his ass.

He was showing me no mercy as he furiously fucked my face! All the hate and disgust he felt toward me was evident in his every thrust! He couldn't know how I loved it!

The muscles of his ass worked faster and faster as he pushed my head down on his cock with greater and greater force! I realized Tony was getting close! I prepared myself for the moment when he would shoot off into my mouth but before I could catch a good breath, TONY SHOT OFF. HOT COME POURED AND POURED INTO MY MOUTH FASTER THAN I COULD SWALLOW IT. I could feel it squirt against the back of my throat and all over the roof of my mouth!

With one last wild lunge, he rammed his burning passion all the way into me, holding my head tight against his sweating crotch! I could feel his balls, hot and damp lying against my neck. My fingers were caught tightly in the crack of his ass like a vise! I feared my stamina would fail me. My lungs burned for want of air!

Just as I thought I would black out, Tony eased up. I gulped a huge lungful of air and felt better immediately. Tony let his cock soak in my mouth for a long time. I enjoyed running my tongue around the head of it, trying to keep the foreskin from closing over it!

I pressed my lips around the base of his cock and pressed tightly as I eased my head back. I extracted a few drops of come by doing this and I did it again and again until there was no more to be had. Eddie and Joe were still with us.

"Hey, Tony," urged Ed. "Push your ass down on his face again. I wanna watch him tongue you!"

"Yeah. But make it fast, Tony," said Joe. "I'm ready for more after watching you!"

Tony made an attempt to raise his ass to where it was over my face again, but just as he did, he lost his balance and rolled over. He lay in a heap next to me. His legs still had me in their grip and I lay there with his wet limber cock in my face. He was too drunk to move. I pulled away from him and dove into the pool.

After a short swim, I opened a can of beer for Tony and helped him back to his shady rock. His trunks lay in a heap at his feet. He was staring at the ground. I knew he was kicking himself for having given in to his passion. His black curly hair fell in a mass over his wide forehead. I turned away so as not to cause him any embarrassment.

I rejoined Eddie and Joe. Joe had that look in his eye and his cock in his hand so I decided to talk fast and maybe he would forget sex for a few minutes!

"Tell me something about this Nancy you mentioned earlier," I asked. "Does she suck you guys off?"

"Only Joe and me," said Ed. "Tony won't go near the pig and she's wild to fuck him!" This made me feel good!

"Is she any good?" I asked. "I mean at sucking cock?"

"Naaa—" said Ed. "She's all teeth. My cock is sore for a week when she's through with me!" I was most delighted to know this.

"Hey, Eddie," said Joe. "You remember Bugsy's face when he shot off?" They both laughed.

"Bugsy had a trump card, see?" said Ed. "And he's making a play and Nancy is under this table sucking him off and just when he's making his play the funniest look comes in his face and he goes 'oh, oh, oh' and he shoots off and throws the wrong card!" Eddie and Joe had a hearty laugh over this. "He not only lost his load but he lost his trump too! Boy! What a night!"

I was aflame with jealousy. I would have given anything to have been under that table instead of that Nancy! Maybe the old girl was dead now, or moved out of the neighborhood—or something! I hoped so!

"You go there often?" I asked.

"Naa," said Ed. "Only when it's cold or raining. I remember the night I brought Hallie with us. Nancy had a fit! She said 'Git that goddamn brat out of here and be quick about it! You kids want me to wind up in the pen or something?' Ha! She sure changed her mind fast when she crawled under the table, eh Joe?"

Hal lay there without moving a muscle. He looked like a statue waiting to be mounted on a pedestal. Joe stood next to me drinking beer. He and Eddie had a mischievous look in their eyes. I didn't trust either of them! They were obviously up to some trickery!

I reached for Hal's belt and undid the buckle. I loved the feel of his firm, smooth stomach muscles. I unbuttoned the fly and opened the flaps. I was very pleasantly surprised to see that he had a full growth of pubic hair. I started to ease his dungarees off and much to my surprise, Hal raised his ass to assist me!

I was totally unprepared for the next instant! What I thought to be a mere fold in the material turned out to be THE BIGGEST COCK I HAD EVER SEEN! I jerked his suit to his knees and stared in wonder at the enormous thing! It stuck out of the blond hair and lay between his magnificent legs, draping itself over a massive pair of balls!

The foreskin didn't cover the head completely and I could see more than half of the deliriously pink head peering out at me! It was totally limber. I knew without measuring that it was a good six and a half inches long!

Eddie and Joe both howled! I don't blame them. I must have looked pretty silly staring down at Hal's big cock with my mouth open and my eyes bulging from their sockets! I felt like a fool. So, I thought, this is what Nancy was spending all her good money for! No one could blame her!

"Whatcha waitin for," laughed Joe. "An invitation?"

"Maybe he's afraid of it! " said Eddie.

"What!" I shrugged. "Afraid of this? Are you two nuts?" I acted as though I had several of this size every day. Actually, I was a little apprehensive about putting my vast experience against anything so massive! But I couldn't let Eddie and Joe know this. I reached for the cock and eased the foreskin back and forth and it began to grow. Seven inches—eight inches— nine inches—would the thing never stop growing!

When I could no longer pull the foreskin over the enormous, throbbing head, I realized the cock had reached its full glory! It was a MASSIVE TEN AND THREE-QUARTER INCHES LONG!

Hal opened his legs a little and his huge balls slid down his magnificent, sweating thighs.

They came to rest on the very rock where his ass lay.

I kissed his knee then ran my tongue up the muscle of his leg and up to his crotch. I ran my tongue over his soft, silky balls and then sucked them into my mouth and devoured the salty sweat that clung to them! I wanted desperately to run my tongue under his balls and into the crack of his ass, but Hal's position made it impossible to do this—I ran my tongue as far down as I could and wiggled it around till I could feel Hal squirm and push against my face. He raised slightly off the rock but couldn't hold his ass in this position long enough for me to do him much good!

I let go of his balls and licked the base of his cock. Then I ran my tongue back and forth the whole length of it. When I had it thoroughly wet, I took the massive head in my mouth and tried to go all the way down on it. It got as far as my throat and refused to go further. I tried again and again, but just couldn't manage it.

I was terribly embarrassed with Joe and Eddie watching me!

"Ya can do better'n that," said Eddie, giving my head a little push.

"Sure!"said Joe.

I let go of the cock for a moment. "Look, junior. Who in hell is doing this, anyway?"

"All right, all right," said Eddie. "I didn't mean nothin'."

"I know you didn't, Eddie," I said. "I just liked this cock so much, I want to work on it for a while."

"I just wanted Hal to feel it like it was sliding up a hot cunt, that's all," Eddie explained.

"Don't worry. He will," I said. But I wonder—I took the head of Hal's cock in my mouth again and did my best, but just couldn't get it down. I wanted so much to be alone with this beautiful boy! By then I couldn't blame my failure on Joe and Eddie. I'd had many an audience in the past, and it never bothered me. Then Joe got into the act.

"For Christ sakes, Pete," he said disgustedly, "and me tellin' these guys what a good cocksucker you was and now you can't even suck Hallie off. What in hell is the matter with ya, huh?"

Joe was right. But, nevertheless, I was pissed off with him for yelling at me.

I picked up Hal's cock and waved it at Joe. "Here, here," I shouted.

"Up your ass with this," and I walked away from them. I threw myself on my blanket and hid my face in my arms.

"Just like Tony said," I could hear Joe saying. "A wise bastard." Then I felt Joe lay down on top of me pushing his cock into the crack of my ass. I pushed him off and jumped to my feet. "Okay Joe," I said. "Lay the hell off!"

What in hell was happening to me anyway? Did I ever turn down a cock—any cock? Hell no!

"I'm hotter'n hell, Pete," pleaded Joe. "Christ, I just gotta get in!" His heart-breaking plea set me afire! I grabbed my oil and wet Joe's cock and helped the head of his cock into me. Ordinarily, it would have taken a lot of patience to get a cock that big into me, but once Joe got the head in, I moved back with a quick lunge and buried it deep! A wild gasp, half pain, half passion broke from my lips! Joe was easing his cock almost all the way out and then ramming it home!

The pain was quickly replaced with the most delicious tingling that gripped my groin and spread like a soothing hand over my entire body.

"Christ, that looks good, Joe!" said Eddie, who had moved in for a closer look. "I wish I did that instead of getting blowed!"

"GET IT UP, EDDIE!" I gasped. "YOU'RE NEXT!"

I pushed against Joe's cock and could feel his wet balls banging against me as he plunged the cock in and out. Eddie stood next to us with his mouth open, trying to jerk his cock to an erection.

Joe rammed his stiff cock deep into me with a powerful jab and shot off. He threw his arms around me and squeezed tight. This was the closest any of them had come to making love to me. I was thrilled!

Joe clung to me for a moment and then started to move his

cock in and out again. I knew he wasn't finished yet. I cooperated with him, matching him stroke for stroke and tightening up as best I could. This tightening up had him off quicker than the first time.

I loved the feel of Joe's big cock pushing in and out of my ass. I hated to have him pull out of me as my quivering body cried out for more cock!

Joe picked up a bar of soap and dove into the pool. Without a word, Eddie jumped on me piggyback! His skinny arms and legs tightened about my body and I could feel his big cock against the crack of my ass! I reached down and eased it in. God! How much bigger than Joe's! It seemed to fill my whole insides! How could I have let that little bastard Joe fuck me when all this cock was here for the taking?

I revolved my ass around frantically and kept the huge thing deep inside me till Eddie shot off. I was a little sorry to have him come so soon, but he damn near had me off. I didn't want to shoot off myself just yet, as I wanted another go at Hal. Eddie joined Joe in the pool and I walked over to Hal. I wondered, as I looked at his huge, limber cock, if I might possibly get all or a good part of it in me. I doubted it, but I was hot as hell and willing to try anything—however mad—at the moment!

I heard Joe say something about taking a nap, and decided to wait till he and Eddie were asleep before trying anything with Hal. I felt strangely shy about having sex with him with people looking on. For some strange reason, I wanted to be with him—alone!

I left Hal on his rock and walked over to the pool. Eddie and Joe were making themselves comfortable on my towel. Tony was fast asleep. His shriveled cock was almost buried in his thick, black hair. I seemed to be the only one awake. I soaped up and swam around for a few minutes. The water was so good— but cold! A movement caught my eye and I was startled to see the magnificent Hal easing himself off the rock. He stood there for a moment, stretching and yawning. Then, with long easy strides, he moved toward the pool where I stood.

His walk was strangely like that of an animal. His huge cock, dark against the intense white of his untanned groin, swung from side to side with every step. There was something magnetic and gripping about him that I couldn't dismiss. Few men had affected me this way!

Despite the cold water, I couldn't dim the hot excitement that gripped and all but enveloped me! Hal stood at the edge of the pool looking very much like a Greek deity! His perfect body was covered with sweat, and his skin glistened like wet marble in the brilliant sun.

He glanced over his shoulder and seemed satisfied that the other boys were asleep. I stood transfixed as Hal spread his legs apart. I could see where his balls joined his body. How I yearned to explore this area with my tongue! I watched, fascinated as he reached down and brought his hand up under his huge cock. He raised it slightly, letting the enormous thing lay in the palm. As I stared at the head of his cock, completely bewitched, a great stream of piss burst through the opening and shot directly at me! It broke the surface of the pool with a shattering splash just two feet from where I stood! I couldn't have moved if he had squirted it straight into my upturned face! I was completely imprisoned by this stunning boy's strange charm.

When he finished pissing, he milked his cock down, squeezing the big drops out. I trembled with excitement when he swung the big thing around, shaking off the drops that clung to the head! Then he dove into the pool and disappeared underwater.

I watched for him to break water, but there was no sign of him. Then I was startled by a voice behind me. Hal had swum underwater completely around and behind me.

"Borrow your soap, mister?" he asked. I loved the sound of his deep voice. This was the first time I had really heard him say anything. I turned around to face him. He stood waist-deep in the pool, but I could see the submerged portion of his body in the clear water.

"Sure," I managed to say. "Turn around and I'll soap you back if you like."

He turned his back to me and my hands moved quickly over the smooth, satiny muscles and then down to his magnificent ass. I felt a strange tingling such as I had never known, run through my body. I could not tear my eyes from his ass! I soaped each buttock and the firm legs beneath them. Hal made no objection when I ran my fingers daringly into the crack. I soaped this thoroughly. He stepped to a higher rock and only the head of his cock hung into the water.

When my middle finger found his asshole I exerted a slight pressure and it felt hot—even in the icy water! I soaped this for an unnecessarily long time and I could feel Hal pushing against my hand. He liked it!

I reached for his shoulders and turned him around without speaking. I soaped him all over, working up a lot of suds as I scrubbed his cock and balls. He had a roaring hard-on now. Pushing away from me, he fell backward into the water. I tossed the soap on the bank and followed him. We swam for a couple of minutes and then Hal found a footing in fairly deep water and stood there watching me.

I went underwater and came up against him. His crotch was in my face and I took his cock in my mouth. I felt his hand gently rubbing the top of my head. I sucked on his cock for a while and then came up for air. The next time I went under I pushed my tongue hard into his crotch. Hal squatted and pushed the crack of his ass firmly into my face. My lungs were bursting for air and when I came up, Hal pushed away and swam for the opposite shore.

He quickly ran into the thick woods and was out of sight before I could follow. I swam swiftly across the pool and followed in the direction he had taken—but he was nowhere to be seen. I was frantic least I lose him! Ahead was a small clearing where the sun broke through the trees and the ground was thick with tall grass. I rushed toward this clearing.

Midway across, I tripped and fell flat on my face! Then I heard a mischievous laugh—low and husky. I realized that Hal had reached out and tripped me as I ran by. He seemed quite pleased with his little trick. I was so relieved to find him that I didn't mind being tripped in the least!

Hal let go of my ankle and lay back in the grass—his hands forming a pillow beneath his head. His eyes were closed against the glaring sun. I looked at him for a long time. I studied the magnificent body and the huge cock and balls. I knew I should never behold such beauty again—ever! Except for the slight movement of his breathing, Hal lay motionless.

Then—as though to get things started, he brought his hands up and placed them on his chest. His fingers dug into his flesh for a moment and then moved slowly down his body to his crotch. He rubbed his cock and balls for a while, then brought his hands back up over his chest, across his face, and stopping behind his head. This little movement obviously excited him as his cock began to get hard.

A passionate desire swept over me! I threw myself upon him and took a mouthful of flesh and sucked it into my mouth till it turned red. Then I moved up and licked and kissed his enormous hands till they trembled. I sought his ears and kissed them and ran my tongue into them till Hal groaned with ecstasy!

My lips followed his hairline, outlining his eyebrows and then running back and forth across his closed eyelids.

I moved my tongue down the side of his face, carefully avoiding his mouth, then began to rain kisses upon his smooth throat!

I sucked on his nipples till they were hard and red! My hands were not idle during this. My left hand caressed his body while the right hand groped wildly in Hal's crotch! Hal's whole body was a twisting, squirming mass now! He was half mad with passion! I bypassed his crotch and licked both legs right to the toes!

With a quick turn, Hal rolled over on his stomach. I showered his magnificent buttocks with wild kisses! Then I tongued the small of his back for a moment and worked my way down into the crack of his ass. Hal sprang into action and raised himself to his knees, presenting me with the best position in which to work on him! I was sobbing with passion and the response from Hal was electrifying! The harder I pushed my tongue against him, the louder he moaned.

I moved my face down and took his huge balls in my mouth. THEY WERE DRIPPING WITH FRESH SWEAT!! Hal rolled over on his side while I sucked on his balls. My finger sought the tight little hole of his ass. Hal groaned when I slipped the tip of my finger into him, so I relaxed for a moment before continuing.

He rolled over on his back. I took the head of his cock in my mouth and ran my tongue over it. I tried to go all the way down on it, but it seemed impossible! Hal was on his elbows now frantically fucking my face. He took my head between his hands and pushed it down hard on his cock. It slid down my throat a little more!

Then Hal raised his legs up on my shoulders and locked them around my neck. He pushed down again, and the enormous cock slid down my throat! As the last inch stabbed into me, he cried out and started to shoot off.

I could feel the HOT COME rushing through his cock and down into me! THE HEAD HAD SWOLLEN TO THE SIZE OF AN ORANGE AS HE CONTINUED SHOOTING-IT WAS THE LONGEST ORGASM I HAD EVER EXPERIENCED! I THOUGHT HAL WOULD NEVER STOP SHOOTING OFF INTO ME!

I felt his body relax and he let go of my head and fell back to the ground, panting heavily! I pressed my lips around his cock and milked every last drop from him!

I loved the taste of the HOT CREAMY FLUID! I regretted not having had the whole load shot into my mouth so I could taste it thoroughly and swallow it.

I realized suddenly that I had gotten my finger all the way into Hal's ass! I could move it in and out with no trouble and no objection from Hal. I tried inserting a second finger. It slid in with some difficulty, but not as much as I might have expected. Then I worked the two around and around inside his ass. I could feel Hal pushing against my hand. His cock was still hard and throbbing in my face, but I was interested only in his ass at the moment. I had to get my burning cock into this magnificent creature even if it meant tying him to a tree to do it!

His legs were still around my neck and he was now pushing with greater force against my twisting fingers. In a flash I moved up on him and put my stiff cock to the crack of his ass and eased it in! We were both so covered with sweat that no other lubricant was necessary!

When the head of my cock slipped into Hal, it felt as though I had dipped it into liquid fire! It was hot and tight and extremely painful! I waited a moment for the pain to subside, then pushed it in a little further. Hal pushed his ass against me and inch by inch my big cock slid into him! I felt completely enveloped by the most intense beauty! The agonizing pain was suddenly replaced with the purest joy!

I reached down and felt my balls. They lay close against his steaming buttocks. I was in to the hilt!

I sucked on his nipples and ran my tongue back and forth across his massive chest. With one hand holding his monumental tool firmly upright in front of me, slowly jacking it off, I employed the other in gently fingering his delicious, silky balls. Hal was a tornado beneath me!

"Fuck me!" he whispered softly. "Fuck me!" I fucked him! With every fiber of my being, I fucked his magnificent hot ass! Before I realized it, I shot off. But no mere orgasm could satiate my hungry desire for this beautiful creature!

"FUCK ME!" He bawled loudly—"FUCKK MEE-E-E!"

His wild cry rang through the still woods around us. I lost all control! Any previous desires to "go easy" with Hal were shot to hell!

Like Tony—I showed Hal no mercy! My whole body was aflame with the fiercest passion I had ever known! With wild, merciless thrusts, I rammed my burning phallus into the quivering dynamo reverberating beneath me! All the longing, the desires and the passions kindling a small flame within me beginning with Joe and working itself up to a white hot inferno with Tony, burst with sudden violence inside Hal and slowly burned itself out!

"Oh, God!" I moaned, as the last of my fury drained into Hal. "Oh Gaaaaaadd!"

I collapsed on Hal and lay there unable to move. I could feel my cock slip out of his ass very slowly. Hal slid out from under me and crawled on my back. I heard him spitting into his hand and then felt the enormous head of his huge cock slide into me! I felt as though my whole body would split in two!

I relaxed as inch after inch slid into me. When I felt his soft, wet balls against the back of my legs, I knew that HE HAD THE WHOLE OF HIS TEN AND THREE-QUARTERS INCHES IN ME! AT THAT MOMENT I KNEW I HAD SCORED MY GREATEST VICTORY!! Hal moved his cock slowly back and forth, in and out of me. I wanted desperately to feel his cock fucking me, so I got to my knees—Hal following my movement without once stopping his steady, deep thrusts. His balls were now slamming against my legs with considerable force!! I reached down and felt his huge cock slide in and out of my ass I was burning with passion! I fingered his balls for a while and then, gently lifting my own balls, began playing with them in my cupped hand.

At this moment I could have let fly with my load of hot cream without touching my pulsing meat at all. I love to do this too: to see a fountain of scalding white juice stream out of my throbbing prick, with no hands touching it, is tremendous. But I also like the feel of a wet, warm hand around my big cock, sliding quickly up and down its thick, slippery shaft; so I fiercely grabbed the eagerly waiting rod and beat off as if I had just invented it.

I could feel Hal's hot breath coming faster and faster against my neck! I squirmed my ass around—pushing it back to make sure that every inch stayed in me when he shot off. With one last savage thrust he rammed it full force into my ass and I could feel THE COME RUSHING THROUGH THE LENGTH OF HIS COCK AS IT POURED INTO ME! I WAS COMING

AT THE SAME TIME AND WE BOTH WERE MAKING A GREAT DEAL OF NOISE!!

I continued to squirm my ass around, even after Hal stopped coming. His face fell to my back, covered with sweat!

His cock seemed endless as it slid slowly out of me. Hal slumped to the ground panting wildly. We lay in the tall grass for a long time.

Hal finally got to his feet and walked back to the pool. I followed him and we both swam across and joined the sleeping boys. Hal lay down next to his brother Eddie and was asleep at once. I snuggled my face against his neck and put my arm over his chest.

I was awakened by a furious jabbing at my asshole. I knew it was Joe just by the feel of his cock. I was so bored and tired of that miserable cock! He shot off quickly and pulled out of me. I was strangely grateful that Hal was not awake to see it.

Eddie woke up and shook Hal and Tony. Then all four boys got up and prepared to leave. I offered them a last beer but they declined. I watched as they put their trunks on and said "so long."

Hal didn't look at me once during this. I felt a terrible loneliness as I watched him slip into his cut-down dungarees. They did take a last cigarette, and then climbed over the rocks and started downstream.

I ran to the edge of the pool and watched them work their way downstream. Eddie was leading with Tony and Joe behind him. Hal followed at a short distance. The three boys in the lead soon disappeared around a rock. I hoped that Hal would turn and wave goodbye to me, but he didn't. He, too, disappeared behind the rock and was gone! I stared at that rock for a long long time.

I decided never to say a word about my good fortune to that miserable bunch of faggots back at camp—that is—at least not till after Labor Day!

It was getting late. I decided to have a last dip before gathering my things together for the long hike back to camp.

And firewood for fried chicken—camp—faggots—and fried chicken—and corn, roasted right in the hot coals—but I didn't feel at all hungry!

CHAPTER NINE
GEORGE

You have never seen a "well put together" in your life until you meet George. George is short, about five feet six inches, with dark hair, and the most beautiful body you have ever laid eyes on. He has just the right amount—and in the right places—of muscles, and he's built like the proverbial brick shit house. I should say, too, that he is much too handsome to be let loose. I sort of gasp for breath every time I think of George, and I think of George often.

George is one of those guys that just sort of naturally brings out the sex in a person. Meeting him is like walking up to a hot stove after you have been half frozen with the cold; or like a tall, cold glass of water after sweltering in the desert all day.

I knew George in college, and he was always surrounded by the most handsome of guys and gals. He certainly had no trouble getting dates and, surprising enough, I don't think he was aware of his sex appeal or good looks. Or at least, if he was, it didn't cause him to be conceited in the least.

Of course I was prejudiced, but it seemed to me that George was more interested in handsome guys than gals. He did date occasionally, but I always felt that he did so for appearances sake rather than from preference. He was a fraternity man and he did have to make some showing in the sexy gal line in order to be "one of the boys."

All the time I knew him I can only remember one gal that he made a big show over, especially around a group of guys. All this sort of proved to me that he was trying to put on an act. It wasn't too convincing either, at least to me.

I might as well relate incidents in my relationship with George. All this is absolutely true. If you don't want to beat your meat, then stop right here. You can't possibly finish this tale with a dry cock. If you are going to continue this story, then my advice to you is to call up your most handsome buddy and invite him over.

I am sure you both will enjoy doing the things I have done with George.

I should start at the beginning when I first met George We were both geology majors at the University of Washington.

It was a beautiful spring day—I could smell the flowers in the air and I really was thinking of fishing instead of attending classes. I was also thinking of going to some secluded spot and lying naked on the soft grass in the warm sunshine. As you can see, sex, if not my first thought was always my second.

But it was the first day of the quarter, so I decided I had better show up. I walked into the sun-drenched room amid a general confusion of conversation and a scurrying around for seats. As I looked around at the mass of faces, I saw George. He was sitting next to a real handsome guy—his buddy.

I sat a couple of rows behind them so I could watch. During that class and many times after that, George would put his arm over his buddy's shoulder and vice versa. It was a tender scene and anyone could tell that they were quite attached to each other. They were always together. You might think that type of action a little too "queer" to be done in public, but with them it looked normal. They were both "butch", and one would figure they were just damn good buddies and a little demonstrative.

I secretly wished I were George's buddy and could receive a show of affection from him. I was a little jealous of the other guy. I was envious of his position in George's life. Up to this time I hadn't even met them, but my imagination was sort of running wild.

I finally got up enough nerve to sit next to George one day

and start talking to him. At first he wasn't as friendly as I wanted him to be, but at least he would always talk to me in the hallways or whenever he saw me on the campus. Every time I would ask him what his rush was, he would always say he had to meet his buddy. I sure wished George would rush to meet me like that.

I wanted to get to know George much better, but didn't know just how to impress him without being obnoxious or appearing too eager. I didn't have too much to in common with him and he usually ran around with his fraternity crowd. If you have ever been in college, you know how difficult it is to break into a fraternity bunch unless you "belong".

One break came sooner than I expected. I saw George in the hall one day and he looked a little downhearted. I very sympathetically asked him what was wrong. He told me his buddy was getting married. I was so happy I could cry—I was a real heel and sort of ashamed of my feelings, but at least I could finally see my chance with George. I sympathized with him and told him I knew what it was like as it had happened to me once.

After that, George's manner toward me was much different. He would always sit next to me in class and we started going places together. I always wanted George, but could never seem to find the right opportunity to try anything. I was awfully shy about those things anyway.

The real beginning of our close relationship came one day when we had lantern slides for a whole period instead of lecture. After the lights were out, George put his left foot up on the seat and his leg touched my arm. I was feeling real bold so I put my arm on his leg with my hand over his knee. I squeezed his knee with my fingers and ran my hand up and down the calf of his leg.

George didn't seem to mind at all, so I kept moving my hand farther up his leg. He started trembling and I figured he was getting excited. My boldness really amazed me, but I was so excited that much of my natural reserve was gone. I lowered my elbow down into his crotch and he trembled slightly. I could feel his stiff cock through his pants. I wanted to take it out and fondle it with my hands and run my fingers over the head and feel it slick with his love juice.

The room, though dark, was much too public a place to do that, but I did reach in with my hand and rubbed his tremendous tool until he was breathing hard and made me stop.

George whispered to me, "Let's go." I was hot enough to burn and I don't think George could take much more either. I was surprised at myself at being so bold, but it sure made a dent in the static situation so far. I had never done anything like this before, but I had a real crush on George and wanted him bad. I didn't know just what George had in mind and I didn't care, so long as it was sex. I was really in sort of a daze—things were happening fast.

I followed George as he quickly walked upstairs and went into a little-used head on the second floor. The booths were paneled solid to the floor, so no one could see us.

As soon as we were inside and the door safely locked, George stripped off his clothes. His tremendous cock was standing at a forty-five degree angle and was throbbing with anticipation. It was at least nine inches long and so big around my fingers wouldn't reach.

George was breathing in short gasps as he fumbled to undo my pants. He motioned to me to get undressed. My own tool was burning with passion and I knew I would come fast, but I held back as hard as I could.

We stood for a few minutes, stripped naked, both with tremendous boners, looking at each other's bodies. George then drew me close and pressed his burning tool hard against my stomach.

He rubbed his huge organ all over my stomach. It felt wonderful—especially after his love juice had lubricated things. That slippery, sliding tool on my trembling body was driving me crazy with passion.

George stopped just before my load was about to go off and we rested a few seconds. When he sensed I was ready again, he placed his tool between my legs from the front and slowly started pushing and pulling until his love juice, which was flowing freely, made things a little slippery. That George really went to town—I can't describe what a thrilling sensation it was to feel that slippery organ plunging in and out of my thighs just below my balls.

My own burning tool was pressed tightly against his stomach, and every time he would thrust his cock in, he would wiggle his body against my hard cock. Electric shocks were running all through me from this passionate exercise. We were both breathing hard now and it would only be a matter of moments before we would shoot our loads. I was surprised I had held on so long.

George finally reached out and grabbed the head of my cock and started jacking me off in rhythm with his fucking. The tempo increased and I tensed. I reached back and felt the head of his cock hit my hand as he thrust in. George shuddered with excitement when he felt my hand, and started to shoot his cream. That got me—my own load spurted out from between his fingers and covered our stomachs and dripped down over our balls onto the floor. George's gorgeous cock was still shooting gobs of cream, and it felt warm and sticky as it flowed freely into my hand and ran down my thighs. Spasms of excitement gripped us as we shot our huge loads onto each other. George gripped me tight and we could both feel the warm fluid oozing between our bodies and down our legs.

We clung to each other this way for a few moments, then separated and surveyed the mess. My legs were covered with George's load as his stomach was with mine. We looked at each other and grinned sheepishly. We were both new at this, and a certain amount of embarrassment was involved.

We cleaned up quickly, using toilet paper, and left the head. When we got downstairs we went outside into the warm sunshine, found a secluded spot under a tree and talked for a while.

George started the conversation; he didn't look at me but

said, "I hope you don't think I'm nasty on account of what happened?"

"Not at all," I replied. "I'm more interested than ever now. I've wanted you ever since I first saw you, but was too damn shy to try anything. I don't know what made me so bold today."

"I'm glad you were," George remarked. "I've been hot for you too, but was afraid to make the first move."

I was feeling very confident by this time, and I continued by asking, "What about your handsome buddy I first saw you with?"

"Oh, you mean Johnny. I had a real crush on him. He taught me everything I know about sex. I didn't think I would ever get over his getting married. But then you showed up about that time and I didn't know who I wanted the most. I'll never forget Johnny though; he really had a piece of meat and was hot all the time. Yours is damn nice too, by the way. We used to go downstairs to the seismograph room and lock the door. It seemed that we would play for hours. He loved to have me massage that ten inch tool of his. I usually ended up blowing him."

George seemed to be willing to talk, so I asked, "What about all those other real handsome kids you go around with. I get hot just looking at them."

"Me too, that's why I like to be around them. They are practically all straight though. Only one I ever had and he made me. You've seen me with that tall, blond, well-built guy? Well, that's Jim, and he is hung like a horse and twice as passionate. He looks real butch and acts that way too, but if he likes you and ever gets you into the bedroom alone, then you are in for a real time."

I coyly suggested, "Maybe we could get together with him some time?"

George grinned at me for a couple of seconds before he answered, "That might be interesting. I've never tried it with more than one. I know another kid in Bremerton. He's sixteen but looks a lot older. He is hot to go all the time. Wants me to play him off every time I see him. Built like a brick shit house too, and a cock on him you could use for a telephone pole. We go swimming lots together," George paused then continued, "nude."

I let out a breath of air and came back with, "You mean this has been going on all the time and I didn't know about it? You're getting me hot again! But I don't care so much about those other guys—it's you I like."

"Thanks, Bud, that's the way I feel about you too. Those other guys are okay, but it's just their bodies I'm interested in. I feel I could be real friends with you."

It is not often you find two guys discussing their affairs and feelings like this, but it was just this type of honest talk that made me feel much more at ease around George. We ended our little talk with George inviting me to spend the weekend at his folk's place on the lake near Bremerton.

I had no idea yet just how glorious a weekend I was in store for. I will never underestimate George's ingenuity again.

I went over on Friday night and George met me at the ferry terminal. During the drive to the lake, George explained that his folks were away for the weekend and we had the place to ourselves. I was glad of that because I'm nervous enough around a strange place without having to make an impression on strange people too.

It was late when we arrived at the lake, so we went directly to George's bedroom. We both stripped and laid on the bed. The full moon was shining bright through the window, and I could see clearly every detail of George's magnificent body.

I reached over and started playing with George's huge tool. It got hard immediately. He then rolled over on top of me and smothered me with kisses as he worked his hot love muscle all over my crotch and stomach. My own cock was burning hot with passion. I finally said, "I can't take much more of this without popping off!" George got up and said, "I'll get something." He returned with a large beach towel which he spread under us.

George then went down on me and started sucking furiously. The thrills I was getting were tremendous. I can't remember when I had enjoyed anything more. Of course, with George, sex is twice as exciting!

I couldn't hold off any longer and I cried, "George, I'm coming!" When he heard this he sucked even more furiously and I shot a load of juice into his mouth that he couldn't hold. It dripped and ran back down over my balls. It seemed like I shot cream for about five minutes, and George kept sucking until every drop was drained from me. We relaxed for a few minutes while I caught my breath.

George then came off of me and stood beside the bed. He was breathing hard and was playing with his cock. He said, "Bud, I've got to get my rocks off!" I swung my legs over the edge of the bed and grabbed George around his bare butt and pulled him close to me. His cock was in front of my face now and I put my mouth over it. I teased him for a while with my tongue. His thrills were intense. He finally cried out. "Faster—faster!" I then went down in earnest and sucked for all I was worth. His body tensed and I could feel the muscles in his buttocks become hard as he rammed his prod forward into my mouth. His load started coming immediately in large spurts. My mouth was full and could hold no more. I had to let it out, and thick gobs of his cream flowed warm down over his cock and balls onto my legs. When his muscles finally relaxed, I came off of him and pressed my head against his stomach. I ran my hands up over the muscles in his back while George gently ran his hands over my shoulders and neck. After a few minutes of this, he playfully ruffled my hair and said, "Let's clean up." We both took a warm relaxing shower and went to bed. We cuddled close to each other contentedly and went to sleep.

We had a late breakfast the next morning. The sky was bright and cloudless and the sun was hot. George was showing me around the place when we heard someone calling George's name. We looked up and saw Jim, the blond guy, hurrying toward us. George had told me before how he and Jim had done each other on several occasions. If it hadn't been for that advance knowledge, I would never have thought that this young blond giant would ever be interested in things like that.

After introductions were over, George suggested that we go for a swim. Jim said that he didn't have a suit with him. George countered with. "That's all right, we won't need them anyway." With that, we three went to the lake shore and piled into a rowboat.

George took off his shirt, exposing his beautiful chest and arms, and started rowing us down the lake. I marveled at George's musculature as he rowed effortlessly, and realized the power in his well-knit body. This was the first time I had ever seen George in a dynamic situation where I could fully appreciate how well built he was.

In a short time we were beaching at a secluded grassy cove.

George said that this place was perfectly private and the only way to reach this spot was by water.

After the boat was secured, George and Jim stripped, revealing man's beautiful body in the raw. I was electrified at the sight of two handsome guys naked—standing before me. I could picture them both together on the cover of "Body Beautiful."

I hadn't realized that I was staring when a shout, "Hey Bud, don't be bashful!" broke into my concentration. I stripped off my clothes and joined them in the water. We swam and played around for about a half an hour. They could both swim like fish and I was a little put out keeping up with them. Most of my swimming usually takes place on the beach soaking up the sun. However, I was enjoying this activity very much. We all came out of the water at the same time, spread a blanket on the grass, laid down to rest and dry off. We laid side by side with George in the middle.

I had almost fallen asleep in the warm sunshine when I felt a hand on my cock. My boner rose immediately. I opened my eyes and saw that George had turned over on his stomach and that it was his hand that was grabbing me. Jim too was on his stomach and had his arm over George's back. Jim raised up and saw what was happening. He exclaimed. "Wow-ee! How long has this been going on? Hey, Bud, have you got a license for that thing?" Jim then got up on his knees where I could see that he had a most gorgeous nine inch boner. It was so big and fat it looked like it was about ready to explode. Jim leaned over, pressing his hard tool onto George's back, and grabbed my joy stick. He massaged it real good and kiddingly remarked, "You know it's against the law to carry a concealed weapon."

I said, "Oh yeah! What about that cannon of yours?"

George couldn't contain himself any longer and pushed up in between us and said, "Hey, you guys! I'm here too." His tool was throbbing with passionate excitement and it was wet on the head where his love juice had come out.

George sat in the middle and grabbed our boners, one in each hand, while we both grabbed his. Love juice was flowing freely from all three of us and the heads of our cocks were quite slippery.

We then took turns sucking on each other's cocks until we were so passionate we were all ready to come. Jim then said, "I don't care which one of you fuck me! I don't know if I can take those poles of yours, but I'll try!"

I didn't know much about fucking so I didn't say anything. George, however, volunteered with, "Okay, bend over!"

I watched as Jim got on his hands and knees while George began working his huge prod into Jim's rear. It was a tight fit and George had to collect love juice from all three of us for lubrication. George finally got it in and began ramming it in and out. Jim squirmed and groaned with pleasure from the thrills he was getting. I looked at George's face and saw his expression of intense excitement. My own tool was burning hot and felt like it was ready to pop off. I felt a little left out, so I slid down underneath Jim so my cock was under his face. He immediately went down on me and I shivered and got goose bumps from the excitement.

I watched as my prod appeared and disappeared into Jim's mouth. Beyond, I could see Jim's immense pole in George's hand. I could feel Jim's weight shift every time George would ram it in. All three of us were being done at the same time and I hoped that this glorious sensation would never end.

Suddenly I felt something warm and sticky spurting on to my legs. I looked and saw that Jim was shooting his load. That beautiful cream really had power behind it and it was coming fast and thick. That set me off too and my load shot into Jim's mouth and some of it was running back down over my cock. George was groaning now too and I knew he was also coming. I could feel some of his cream dripping down on to my legs which were directly under Jim's butt. It was a thrilling sensation for all three of us to relieve our passion at the same time.

After the excitement died down, we all went back into the lake and cleaned ourselves off. For the first time in my sex life, I had an almost perfect sensation of contentment. After Jim went home, George commented on what an interesting time we had. It was the first "gang bang" either of us had experienced.

Aside from sex, George was a friendly, lovable guy that I wanted to be around all the time. George also seemed to prefer my company. Jim, although extremely good-looking, seemed to play the "Lone wolf;" consequently his greatest attraction was purely sexual.

That weekend went much too fast, but we had school to think of. My mind wasn't always on school; I couldn't ever forget the thrill of my experiences with George. Every time we would get together it would seem even more passionate and enjoyable than the last time. Every day that went by I liked George more. Practically all of our free time was spent in each other's company.

Our close friendship wasn't a possessive thing. We both realized that each had a life to live and that jealousy could only drive us apart. Neither of us objected to the other having a sex affair with someone else, but when we were together we just didn't want anything but each other. It was truly the most satisfying arrangement for both of us.

George and I frequently discussed the affair we had with Jim. It kept popping in our minds at the oddest times. I think that we were ready for another round of "gang bang" but wanted someone else instead of Jim. The opportunity came unexpectedly one day when George came rushing up to me with an excited look on his face and said, "Boy, am I really shook! That mother trout really had me fooled!"

"Mother trout" was one of George's favorite expressions and it could mean just about anything, so I asked, "What do you mean?"

"Well," continued George, "you know that good-looking guy, Paul, who shares a room with me at the fraternity house? Guess what? I walked in on him today and caught him jacking off!"

"Very interesting!" I replied. "What happened?"

"Well, he was awfully embarrassed at first, but I sat down and talked to him for about an hour and guess what?"

"You tell me—I'm not good at guessing." was my reply.

"He said that he has wanted me ever since he has known me! Boy, was I really shook! You know I've been interested in him too. And that cock of his! Whee!" George indicated with his hands the size, and it looked more like a fisherman lying about his catch.

I let out a sigh and said, "Are you thinking the same thing I am?"

"You bet I am," was George's answer. "I've already invited him over to the lake for the next weekend. You're coming too, aren't you?"

"I wouldn't miss it; I'll be there Saturday morning."

"Okay," George replied. "That's when Paul arrives too."

When I arrived Saturday morning, Paul and George met me. They had already decided to go on a hike in the mountains to a hot lake. What I didn't already know was that George had also invited a sixteen-year-old Adonis—Norman. George had told me before that he and Norman had been playing around with each other, but I had never met Norman. However, it wouldn't make any difference as George always knew that anyone he had an affair with would be my type too. And I knew that anyone George had an affair with was something special. I was anticipating the glorious time we would have.

I had met Paul before at school. He had dark, crew cut hair and a beautiful build. His resemblance to Robert Wagner, the movie star, was striking. At first I had mistaken him for Robert until he finally proved he wasn't. He told me one time when he was in Hollywood on a vacation, people would stop him on the street and ask him for his autograph. It is amazing how much two people can look alike and not be related.

Norman was one of the cutest, curly headed, young men I had ever seen. He did look older than his sixteen years, and he was really built. You could tell he had spent lots of time in the sun as his smooth skin was tanned to a golden shade. He would look exciting in the swim trunks and more exciting without.

We finally got under way and drove for about an hour to a spot in the Olympic Mountains where the trail led to the lake. It was a natural hot lake and the water was just pleasantly warm. It took us about an hour and a half to reach the lake. George was also a photo fan and that was the reason he picked this spot--otherwise we could have gone to the other spot on the lake where George lived. The mountains were always beautiful and the air exhilarating. By the time we reached the lake on this warm day, we were ready for a relaxing swim. I was glad that no one was there ahead of us, but we did find a secluded spot for our swim.

George, Norman and I immediately started to strip. I got a good look at Norman as he slowly revealed his body. He was even better built than I had imagined. When he took off his shorts I got the surprise of my life. That boy really had a hunk of meat that would choke a horse. It looked like a long, fat sausage, and it was soft. I thought to myself that he would never be able to fuck any of us with that prod.

We were all in the water when we turned and looked at Paul. He was still fully clothed—shoes off, that was all. We kidded him and said he couldn't swim with his clothes on. He slowly undressed—he was a little shy, but today would bring some changes in him.

I pretended to swim, but my eyes were on Paul's every move. He undressed so slowly that it was tantalizing. He got his shirt off, revealing a magnificent chest—not massive as with weight lifters, but trim. His broad shoulders tapered down to a narrow waist. He had dark hair on his chest and a little on his stomach. His pants finally dropped. It is hard to say that a man's legs are beautiful, but his were very well proportioned. At last his shorts came off and he stood naked, gleaming in the bright sun. I wished I could have had a photograph of that! George was right; his cock was large and uncircumcised. I could see the shape of the head through the foreskin. It dangled enticingly as he walked slowly to the water. My boner was rising at this glorious sight. George was close by and he grabbed my cock under the water and said,

"Steady, boy."

The spell was over when Paul dove in the water and started swimming. We all enjoyed the relaxing warm water. We stayed in for about half an hour.

We all came out of the water and laid on the grassy bank in the warm sunshine and relaxed. I began to feel drowsy, but didn't want to go to sleep. I was interested to see how this party would get under way.

I raised my head to see how things were and really got a surprise. Norman was on his back with his eyes closed but he had the most tremendous boner I had ever seen. I swear it was eleven inches long and it reached up past his navel. I was on my stomach and my tool became stiff immediately when I saw that. George was on his stomach too and might have been asleep, but not for long, because I got up and laid on top of George, placing my boner in the crack of George's butt. I reached over and grabbed Norman's tool. He didn't move, so I knew he had been expecting someone to do that. I said, "If the telephone company needs any spare poles I will tell them about you."

At the sound of my voice Paul opened his eyes and saw what I was doing. He was lying on his back and it didn't take long for his tool to swell up to about ten inches. He looked a little embarrassed, but he grinned at me and said, "Let me feel it too." There was plenty of room on that meat for two hands.

George, always kidding, said, "Okay boys, save some for me." It wasn't long before each had someone's tool in his hand massaging like mad. This went on for a couple of minutes until Norman wanted someone to fuck him. I'm glad he didn't want to fuck any of us with his piano-leg cock. Beautiful to look at and go down on, but not to be screwed with.

George obliged and Norman got on his hands and knees with George behind ramming the meat to him. I started doing a sixty-nine with Paul. In a few minutes we were all ready to shoot our wads. I told Paul that it would be more interesting if we all got together. I slid down, as before, so that my cock was under Norman's face. He sure latched on to my tool fast—like a hungry calf. I motioned to Paul to straddle my waist. He did, and soon I was sucking furiously on Paul's huge cock. I knew that George was jacking Norman off, but couldn't watch.

The excitement was so great that I was ready to pop my juice. Soon Norman's hot cream began spurting and flooding onto my legs. That's all I was waiting for; I let loose of my load and it went like a skyrocket into Norman's mouth. Paul sensed the excitement and started coming with a flood of nectar into my mouth. George was coming too—I can always tell—he gives a short groan when he pops off. Norman's load kept spurting onto my legs and I thought he would never quit. That guy had a load to match his eleven inches of cock. My legs were literally covered with hot, sticky cream, and still he pumped more. Paul was no slouch either—I couldn't take all his load, and it ran out of my mouth, warm and juicy onto my neck.

That Paul really sexed me up. His remarkable resemblance to Robert Wagner had much to do with it I'm sure. This was just as good as having Robert, but I wondered if Robert had as beautiful a tool.

We finally finished and went back into the lake to clean up. I was the one who needed the cleaning most.

I saw Paul several times after that and we really enjoyed

ourselves. I remember one time when George and I were with Paul, driving around in George's car. Paul was so hot that day that he took our cocks out of our pants and we took a side road to a secluded spot. We went into the woods a ways and stripped down naked. I watched Paul as he gave George a blow job. He took George's nine inch cock all the way down, and when George went off, cream spurted everywhere. The reason for this was that just as George was coming, Paul came off him and did the rest by hand. I swear George's load had gunpowder behind it, as it seemed to shoot two feet straight up in to the air. Sort of like "Old Faithful" in miniature. I could hardly stand the strain any longer—I was dripping love juice by the spoonful. George then took on Paul, but Paul's love muscle was a little too long to go all the way into George's mouth. I got up close where I could watch Paul's tool slushing in and out. I was, by this time, fit to be tied and was jacking off. I started coming all over Paul's stomach. When Paul felt this, he started coming in George's mouth. George had to let go as he couldn't take any more cream and jacked the rest of it off, so for a couple of moments Paul and I were mingling our hot cream on his stomach. Paul later told me that was the sexiest thing he had ever felt when my load started hitting his stomach. I admitted I enjoyed the sensation too.

There were other times and other affairs, mostly with George. I'll bet we tried everything in the book and then invented a few more. I'll leave the rest of those experiences for another story. In the meantime, since George and I are separated, we write to each other quite often and I plan a visit with George real soon. We sort of lost track of Paul, but as I said before, George and I are real close buddies and our interest in each other has never diminished. In fact I can think of nothing better than being with George, either in or out of bed.

PART FOUR
A BIT(E) OF THE OLD S & M

The following group of stories is again unusual, by virtue of the subject matter. They deal with sadomasochism in its various forms. This alone would make them a bit different, such material being less readily available than most. It would be sufficient to make them valuable as well, not only to collectors and devotees of such activities, but to the serious sexologist as well. For all that we may read and study about the sadist, nothing can give us quite the same electrifying glimpse of the workings of his mind as can his own fantasying. And it is clear enough that the writers of these pieces are writing about their own special pleasure. The story of the urolagniast is by a urolagniast and he has, as it were, opened the doors upon his inner thoughts and feelings. We see him, as we see his fictional characters, stripped bare. We may not enjoy the sight—but we can appreciate its value.

Of all these tales, Unsexed is surely the most unusual, and may be the most unusual story written. It is worthy of de Sade; indeed, there is more than a casual resemblance. The subject matter is one rarely if ever treated in this manner—that of castration. From time to time castration, usually symbolic, occurs in "fuck stories". The author or narrator becomes a woman, used by rampant males. But the urge to castrate others is surely one of the most rare of deviations, and no other Tijuana Bible story has been found that deals with the same subject. After all, it is to this part of his anatomy that the author of such tales is appealing.

Navy Boot Camp would seem from its title to belong in the chapter devoted to military stories. But while the story takes place at a Navy barracks, its subject matter demanded that it be placed here. This is a tale of dominance, plain and unvarnished; master and slave, sadist and masochist, torturer and punished. We are not certain which of the two principle characters the author identified with—probably the masochist, or rather, the slave. But the workings of the sadistic mind are well depicted, and the story reads like a catalogue of humiliation.

Salty Ship Mates again suggests the military chapter; moreover, it smacks of bisexuality, as two lusty young sailors are encountered by a man and a woman in a bar, and attend a party with boys and girls. But despite his protestations to the contrary, it is his companion, Claude, who most interests our hero, and while he may prattle about getting into "Betty's twat," he derives more pleasure from having his "prong nipped" underwater by Claude.

But without preamble, the party which our young friends have attended becomes a flagellation club meeting, and we get to "the meat" of the matter. The matter, it turns out, is an incredible display of unique sexual practices, all sadistic or masochistic, from licking champagne from bodies, to flinging ping pong balls at erect penises. Golden showers and golden screws, and combinations of the two, are amply described; wine flows down the back, the buttocks, and thus over the inserted penis to provide a buggering pair with new thrills; and hormone martinis seem the logical fuel for these weird fires.

It is hardly surprising that *Taking a Piss* concerns itself with behavior of the uro-complex, or "golden shower" variety, moreover, the copro-complex of behavior concerned with excrement and feces. We step into the mind of the slave, and are horrified and strangely fascinated by his debasement. We are moved too by his bittersweet recognition of what dwells within him—"...I have nothing to say about it and will probably like it. And I guess I do, kind of."

Tortured With Sex carries the same theme forward, from the point of view of the sadist or master—in this case, two masters. But strangely, although it is longer and in more detail, it horrifies less. Perhaps we sense that this author's heart is not in it. Dominance is his scene, but the pain is not so much as we might expect, and the care taken to avoid bruising or cutting suggests only a half-hearted wickedness.

Leather Fun boils down to that—a leather fetishism which pretends to a throne of sadism, but fails to convince. It had little to offer in the way of entertainment, literary value, charm, even little sexual stimulation. But it is an interesting example of the obsession with leather that is typical of many homosexual groups. Leather—leather—leather—black leather—soft leather—hard leather—shiny leather...the words trip over themselves in repetition, often in the same sentence. The narrator is literally smothered in it.

Taken as a whole, these six stories offer a virtual primer in the workings of the sadistic, masochistic and leather-fetishistic mind. Entire volumes could be written—have been written—on these subjects. But it is within reason to suggest that one will come closer to understanding these strange phenomena from reading these few pages than from poring over the weighty tomes of the "experts". For all their fantasy, for all their fictionalization, these are real stories, about real people.

CHAPTER TEN
UNSEXED

One Sunday morning I arose very early and tiptoed down the upstairs hallway. The purpose was to investigate what went on in my house. I had been left with the problem of a ward, a boy, offspring of a servant who had died in my employ. Why I had undertaken to raise and educate this brat, nice as he was remained a great mystery. Frank had become the horror of my life with his licentious depravity, no doubt inherited from his tart of a mother, or from his father, whoever he may have been.

After her untimely demise, I discovered that she had never been married at all, despite a stream of lies she had fed to me over a period of years. It was impossible to locate even a single relative of this wanton, whom I had trusted. The blood of illicit passion flowed freely in the veins of the youth and in spite of everything I could do it was impossible to prevent him from amusing himself sexually with any girl he could find.

Quietly, I opened the door of Frank's room and as I had suspected, there was Frank pumping away on top of the young daughter of my cook. He had nothing on and she also was nude. Their arms were about each other and they were kissing, absolutely lost in a wild fit of depraved lust. It was not the first time I had caught him in such a situation, for he had been corrupting himself for two years. I threw the door wide open and marched in, thinking he was such a nice boy to be doing this dreadful thing. He was a delight to all who knew him, just fifteen, beardless as a girl, with a soft, low pitched voice. In fact he was such a good-looking youth as to make quite an impression on me, but I resolutely kept the secret. I would have gladly taken that beautiful cock. But no—here in front of me was this sight, his young cock, almost as big as any I had seen—it looked as hard and smooth as ivory, and I was forced to fix my attention on its rapid, pushing and withdrawing motion, which she seemed to encourage and meet by the heaving of her ass to every rapid shove.

I felt awfully agitated and all of a rage—Frank and this slut... and how they seemed to enjoy it; they clung to each other in ecstasy, and the lips of her cunt seemed literally to cling to his shaft, holding on and protruding in a most luscious manner at each withdrawing motion, but it soon came to an end and both jumped up in bed as if a bolt had thrown them up. They stared at me wild-eyed. "Disgusting!" I said, and then, "How dare you do this in my house! I shall have you both thrown out. Come to my room at once, Frank—and you, whore, get out and never come back again!" I turned and left the room, went directly to my room, and sat on the sofa, my blood beating in my temples as I thought of what I should do with this boy.

Ever since I was a small child, I had dreamed of cutting a man's penis off.... Now being a grown man, the idea still stuck with me, but I was old enough to know better...I thought of this as I waited for Frank and I thought of his cock.... Yes...how would it be to have one's tool removed completely.... Yes...that is an idea.... It would be dangerous to fool around with here in the U.S., but if the crime was committed in Europe and by an experienced doctor.... Food for thought!

Frank entered with bowed head; he was a young stud, only fifteen, and as yet no hair on his body except for a luxurious patch of blond hair around his cock and balls. I addressed him firmly. "Your mother worked for me for years, and now she is dead and you have nowhere to go, or no relatives to take care of you. I feel that I am due the proper respect from you."

Frank answered: "Yes, sir, you are my guardian, and I always want to show you the greatest respect."

"Indeed," I exclaimed. "What you and that girl were doing just now, I suppose is respect."

"We didn't mean any harm, sir, I'm sorry", said Frank quietly, "we won't do it again."

"I certainly hope not," I said, dismissing the boy for the time being. I went to my desk and took up pen and ink and wrote the following letter to a friend of mine who lived in Paris. My friend was a famous procurer of boys who had only the best working for him. I had worked a little for him while in Paris just for the kicks. Most of the boys did just that: just for the kicks—like being professional whores.

Dear Mr. Dupre,

I am writing this in the hopes that you may be able to do me a big favor. And I shall repay you, very generously. The favor I wish is, that you find a doctor somewhere in Paris who is willing to remove the external organs of a fifteen-year-old boy (his penis and testicles), who is in my charge.

Of course the above operation will have to be done with the utmost secrecy, as it is against the law to have this type of operation performed in the United States.

Thanking you for your consideration in this matter, I beg to remain.

Yours truly,

Martin Burton

I quickly posted this letter for France. A few days later I received an answer to my letter from my friend in France, and it read as follows:

Dear Martin,

So nice to hear from you—your request is most odd, but understandable. Being in the type of business I am, I know the human mind pretty well, and this is a form of sadistic delight which you are at the moment anticipating.

I found just the person to do the operation; a doctor, who is still young and very good-looking...he is thirty-two years old. Also he had performed this type of operation before, especially on some of the type of men who would rather be girls. He has studied this part of the body quite thoroughly, and I'm sure can carry out your wishes to the letter. There is no law against this type of operation here in France, that anybody knows about. But some of the more popular doctors do require an indication before performing it.

I have made an appointment for next week, and hope that you can make it, as the doctor will be prepared on a certain day for this special job. His fee is high. In U.S. money, it will cost you $5,000, but he promises to carry out the operation in the manner which you suggest.

Sincerely,

Mr. Dupre

I licked my lips in savage sadistic, anticipation. I rang for Frank; he had been very bashful, and quiet lately...so I said: "Frank, I am taking you to Paris on a trip with me. I'm going to have some business to attend to in Europe."

"Oh, thank you, sir, that is very nice of you. I would be happy to go with you to Paris. I've heard so much about it."

"Well, I hope that you enjoy it. Now be a good boy and make sure that you are packed and ready for the trip; I'll make reservations for tomorrow, well leave in the morning."

We took a hotel in Paris, and I left Frank in the room while I went to visit with Mr. Dupre. As I got out of the taxi in front of the house, Mr. Dupre came running down the way and shook hands vigorously with me. "I'm glad you've come. Come on in and let's talk." We entered the house and went into the library, and he asked as we entered, "Where did you leave your charge?"

"At the hotel," I answered.

"Tell me about him," he begged. And I told him every little detail, even my innermost feelings about the operation I had in mind for Frank.

"Why don't you sell him to me? After you have him castrated. I could use him. As you know, I have only the rich visiting me here, and they're always begging for something unusual."

"Why, whatever would you do with the boy, especially a gelded one?" I said.

"I will teach him the art of satisfying men, and by the time he is twenty years old, I'm sure he'll be more girl than boy. I'll teach him how to suck cocks of even the oldest men and make them come. Also how to take it in the ass, and by and by if it ever is possible, perhaps, sometime in the future, it will be possible to really make a girl out of him."

"It will be dangerous," I said.

"Nothing is dangerous pertaining to sex in France. You should know that. Why, a man with a cock as big as a stud horse can go out and pick up little ten-year-old boys, and screw them, for a price."

Then I said, "How much will you give me for him?"

"I should say a thousand dollars would be fair price for him," answered Mr. Dupre.

"A thousand dollars," I laughed. "Why, I could get more than that down in Pig Alley, and you know it. The price will be ten thousand dollars and you take all responsibility," I said coldly, for I was rather angered over this greediness.

"My God, ten thousand dollars," suffered Mr. Dupre. "I can offer—and this is my very best—six thousand dollars, and I'll probably have to ship him to Arabia to get my money back."

"I don't give a damn where you ship him to. I'll take the six thousand—and have it ready the day after the operation. I'm not going to be beat out of that." I answered.

"It's a deal and I wouldn't want him any other way. Yes, you have him emasculated. Just don't have anything done with his buttocks; my customers like nice asses," replied Mr. Dupre.

Mr. Dupre gave me the address of the doctor, which was located out in a beautiful district. He lived in the Villa Sayr, a mile or more from any other resident. I dismissed the taxi, and entered the gate, which was unlocked. I had called the doctor, and had an appointment with him, so I was sure of meeting him here at his home. As I pushed the metal gate open, a bell rang on the front porch, and the front door opened. To my surprise, a most handsome man, with a good build, stood there smiling, with outstretched hand, and I said, "I am Mr. Burton, from America. I think Mr. Dupre has okayed me."

"Yes, he did, and if he hadn't have. I shouldn't have invited you out over the phone. One has to be careful, and I am especially careful, as I do any type of surgery and I have almost every type of instrument for surgery. Come on in," he said, as he led me to the library.

A cute little Chinese boy brought drinks, which I enjoyed tremendously. It certainly refreshed me. The doctor's hands fascinated me, and I said, "You have the most beautiful hands I've ever seen."

"Why, thank you; I treat them with care, as a life may depend on them," he said. "Why do you wish this work done?" he asked. "Mr. Dupre explained that you wished him castrated."

"Are you trying to get some legal reason for performing this operation, or do you just want to satisfy your own curiosity?"

"Just my own curiosity, Mr. Burton. Don't worry, I wish to perform this operation, and it is as good as done. Just bring him out here."

"Fine," I said. "I was beginning to think that you were just another legal doctor. There is no reason for having this operation done, with the exception, that I found this boy having intercourse with a girl."

"An excellent reason, Mr. Burton," said the doctor. "Do you wish an anesthetic used?"

"No, no that would take all the fun away, I'm afraid," I answered.

"Now we are getting somewhere. I only wanted to know these things, that I do exactly as you wish, as you are paying the bills for this operation, and I always like to do a good job for the one paying me," exclaimed the doctor.

"Good," I said. "I'm happy that I know just what you think. I shall be able to do it for you according to your satisfaction."

"Fine, and when shall I bring him out here?" I asked.

"At your very earliest convenience. Now if you have no other plans, I shall loan you a car, and you can run to your hotel in Paris, and fetch him out and we can get started with the operation by ten-thirty this evening."

I took the car, and drove dangerously fast back to Paris. Arriving at the hotel, I left the car with the doorman, and told him to hold it a few minutes, and I would be right down. I hurried up to Room 416, and entered. I saw that Frank had had dinner, and was reading some comic books. "Come on, Frank, we're going to a party, and you're invited." This fine treatment astonished him, but he got his jacket and soon we were on our way.

I drove like a fiend through the evening to the house of the doctor. "This is it," I said, as I turned into the driveway leading to the garage, beside the house. "Funny-looking place," said Frank, "but don't think I'm not appreciative, Mr. Burton." As we entered the house, I told the doctor, who was now dressed in a white smock, that I would appreciate a drink, as my nerves were a bit frayed. The doctor pulled a cord hanging from the ceiling along the archway, and immediately appeared a Chinese fellow, very husky, in his middle twenties, carrying my drink. "Fu, please entertain this boy here, while I talk with Mr. Burton."

"Will do," he said. The man in white led me down a

passageway and opened a door with a key, and held it open for me to enter. It was an operating room, and it consisted also of two male nurses, in their early twenties. The doctor closed the door and said to the two nurses. "Please prepare," and to me, "are we ready?" I agreed, and he called the houseboy to escort Frank into the operating room.

In a moment they entered. The houseboy had a hammer lock on Frank; his right arm twisted up high on his shoulders behind his back. After he showed him into the room, he released him saying. "Had to use force on the boy, he didn't want to come."

The doctor turned to the cowering Frank, and said. "You may take off all your clothes now."

"No, I won't," said Frank.

"Make him," he directed the houseboy.

The houseboy punched Frank in the stomach with his fist, a short jab, but hard enough to cause Frank to fold up, with both arms over his stomach in pain. "Take off clothes, like doctor say, or I give you more," ordered the husky houseboy. Frank didn't have to be told a second time by the houseboy. Off, a little reluctantly and somewhat embarrassed, came his jacket, shirt and trousers. At his shorts he hesitated just a minute, and the houseboy squeezed the crotch of the Jockey shorts hard, giving a grin. Frank winced at the pain, and quickly shed the T-shirt and slid his shorts over his hips, and dropped them to the floor. Then he leaned down and began to unlace his shoes. "Faster, faster," said the houseboy, as he inserted his finger in Frank's asshole and jabbed. Frank, startled, didn't know if he should leap away or take his shoes off more quickly to end the torment. He decided to endure the finger up his ass and get the shoes off. He took them off, along with his socks, then stood there quite naked, and as he straightened up, the doctor ordered him on the table just as the two male nurses reentered the room. The two nurses had the young boy on the table in a jiffy; his arms were strapped to the sides of the table; a wide strap ran across the small of his back and held him firmly face down on the table; his two ankles were fastened to the edge of the table. Then they turned a crank which caused the table just under his hips to elevate, jutting his ass up and in a good position for examination. The two nurses stood on each side of the table and each took a buttock, pulling them wide apart, to reveal the boy's little brown asshole. The doctor then slipped his finger in and out and said, "Well, my little man, you had better get to like the feel of this, because this is the only way you'll be having sex from now on."

"Oh, please stop—that hurts, please!"

"Stop your sniveling, boy; a strong cock is bigger than a finger, and you're going to have plenty of them up there, so I will give you a helping hand to get you started in accommodating them." With that he produced a long rubber tube resembling a cock; attached to the end was a large rubber bulb. He pushed it slowly into the asshole. Frank squealed in pain.

"Shut up, you brat," said the doctor, and then began squeezing the rubber bulb. The tube up Frank's ass began to expand and become rigid, just like a cock getting a hard-on. When it reached a size of a good ten inch hard-on, the doctor began fucking Frank's asshole with it. Frank screamed, pleaded, begged for mercy, but to no avail. Finally, tiring of this sport, the doctor removed it, with one slow steady movement, and Frank relaxed.

The two male nurses then released Frank, and turned him over on the table and secured the bonds in the same fashion, except they fastened his ankles under the table. Again, the crank was turned, and his hips jutted up, legs spread wide apart, and his pretty cock and balls fully exposed. He kept asking over and over, "What are you going to do to me?" Then the doctor took his penis in his hand and said, "I'm just going to remove this naughty thing; I'm sure you will be better off without it."

Frank started yelling for help, and crying out. "No, no, you can't do that—Mercy. Mr. Burton, tell him to leave me alone—don't let him cut me there."

"Why, Frank, I'm the one that ordered it done to you. I really think you'll be better off without it. Sex is such a crime with girls, and you apparently won't play with boys," I answered with a sadistic smile.

"I won't do that again with girls, not ever again.... Don't do this to me, I beg you; I swear I won't do anything like that ever again," pleaded the boy.

"Then you won't need it ever again. After all you can squat to piss." I said.

In the meantime, the doctor and two male nurses were getting certain instruments ready. He took a loop-like banjo wire and looped it over the penis and nuts, and drew it very tight. Then he pulled outward. The boy really had a good-sized root on him, and I got hot as hell as I watched. Finally he doctor unloosed the loop and removed the wire, saying, "I just wanted to see the size of it: that is the best method of getting the correct size of a soft penis." Then he turned to one of the nurses, a redhead, and ordered. "Shave him; you must get every bit of hair off." The redhead took a straight-edged razor and began to scrape off the hair over his penis, then he scraped up and down on the penis, the boy pleading as he did so. "Please be careful not to cut it."

"You shouldn't care about a little nick with this razor—there's going to be a much bigger cut there as soon as I get this thing cleaned of all the hair," said the redhead.

He finished finally, leaving his crotch reddened from the dry scrapping, then he took some cotton which he wet down good with a boric acid solution. He cleaned the shaved parts thoroughly, and seemed reluctant to release the young cock when the doctor told him that that would do.

"Tongue his penis a little, Bill," the doctor ordered the other nurse, as he slipped the silver banjo wire over the penis and nuts again. Without any prompting, Bill went to work with a satisfied gleam in his eyes. He took the limp penis in his mouth and began working his tongue around over it, as the doctor said to Frank, "Now this isn't so bad, aren't you enjoying it?" The fright went out of Frank's eyes, and he began to work his hips about as much as he could under the restraining straps holding him securely to the table. And as he did so, his penis went up into a hardened good-sized cock, and Bill was working his head up and down now quicker. As the boy started to groan, the doctor pulled tight the wire, pulled it as tight as his strength would permit. The wire seemed to tighten but not loosen; it locked itself, and held onto its hold. The man stopped sucking on the young penis now. Frank was suffering with the pain of his cock being squeezed, cock and nuts, for the wire was right against the body. As I learned later, the cock could not get soft either, as long as all blood was shut off and left inside the penis.

He turned loose the wire now, and as I watched closely, he took up a knife, the name of which I cannot remember. But it was a little medical knife, perhaps four inches in length, and a half-inch wide, and sharper than a razor. He inserted it under the bag, and started slicing neatly, carefully, cutting veins, muscles, tendon, right up through the bag, carefully keeping the knife close to the body. Frank had been fairly quiet, only trembling slightly, until the knife had gone half through the sack. Then: "Eeeee! Ohhhh, God! God! What are you doing to me! Eeeeee wawawawawa! You're really cutting me! Oh! Oh! No! No! Please don't!" We paid no attention, but continued with the operation; the doctor had cut through the bag, and was now slicing carefully through the penis, carefully keeping the blade close to the body. He sliced slowly, ever so slowly. Blood was running down his buttocks onto the table, and was splattering onto the floor. As he cut the last of the penis loose from the body, he threw the whole thing into a pan that had been placed close by on a table on wheels for that purpose. He worked quickly now. He took a smooth silver looking iron from Bill: it had a handle with an electric cord leading from it to the socket in the wall. Quickly he rubbed this over the bloody blot, back and forth. Then I realized what it was. It was an electric heating iron used for this purpose to stop the flow of blood. Frank had already fainted, and was spared this extra pain as he burned his flesh with a burning iron, but surprisingly enough, it did stop the blood flow, and also made it possible for him to open the pee hole and insert a rubber tube. He explained that he didn't dare let any of his urine get on the sore spot, as it might cause an infection. The piss would pass through the little rubber tube. Then he packed the crotch around the hose. He worked frantically for over an hour and forty-five minutes.

I looked at the now limp penis, lying in its own blood, and examined it thoroughly and now know things about the penis that I would never have known if I hadn't witnessed the operation. I still have the penis and balls preserved in a jar, and once in a while when I show my trophies, I take them out, for better viewing of my friends.

The boy is perfectly healthy today, and working as stated before, in a house specializing in very unusual, and different gay sex. The boy healed quickly. It took two weeks for him to be up and about and begin learning his new trade, sucking cock and being fucked in the ass.

CHAPTER ELEVEN
NAVY BOOT CAMP

The Navy boot camp barracks began to stir just going on dawn. A few early risers began to stir sleepily before the bugle even sounded and made for the head. Some squatted in the crapper and some went straight into the showers. Three of them rounded the corner to the urinal set back from the main wash-room. Two of them wore scivvy shorts and one already had his half-hard cock out as he approached. The third wore nothing but the towel over his shoulder, and he scratched his large hairy balls as his fully hard cock waved unabashedly in the air.

All three stopped dead in their tracks at the sight that greeted them. The urinal consisted of two tiled surfaces. One extended out along the floor about three feet, while the other went up the wall about four feet. The two formed a sunken drain flowing from both ends toward the middle. Lying in the drain on his back was a naked man bound hand and foot. A large crudely made sign on the wall over him announced in large hand-drawn lettering: *"This son-of-a-bitch was caught sucking cocks here last night—piss on him good!"*

"So you didn't get enough last night? Well maybe here's something you'll like even better!" The naked boy grinned in contemptuous glee as he pointed his stiff cock down at the man before him. His full bladder made it difficult for him to piss, but soon the long slit at the end of his cock parted and a full stream of hot amber water shot down on the naked body. The first flood landed on the man's limp cock and splashed all over the rest of his body. The contact of the hot tingling liquid started the soft cock to throbbing and swelling, and soon it stood straight up, jerking convulsively in the air.

The most fun was to try to send the whole spurt squarely into the man's open mouth and watch his Adam's apple jump when he tried to swallow the strong pungent stuff. Suddenly the naked man gave a sharp gasp and grasped his cock firmly just as it spurted with flying white jets of creamy juice which splashed over the man's face. This astounding sight drew the other two into a frenzy and they grabbed their cocks and with just a few rapid strokes were soon adding their hot juices to the rain of virile manhood pouring down on the naked man's body.

His body quivering with excitement, and his face flushed with crimson in humiliation of the depths of degrading position and depravity of his own enjoyment of this filthy treatment, his own body suddenly convulsed in violent orgasm as his jerking prick gushed with his own cream which shot back over his body to mix with that of the frenzied young sailors.

Other young sailors were gathering now, their faces flushing with excitement as they read the sign and gazed at the frantic picture before them. The braver ones pushed through, cock in hand, for a position to join the exciting game. As soon as one finished, another took his place, and the naked man was receiving a continuous shower of piss and jism. A mob hysteria spread through the throng of young sailors, and hardly a one failed to be swept into the game. Many hardly got to piss on the helpless man at all, before their excitement set off an explosive spray of hot cream. Some of the lustier ones returned a second time and one naked boy with a trim wiry body, stayed to empty his bladder and throw three full loads of jism into the rain of mixed juice.

The electric wave of passion subsided as quickly as it began, and they all slunk shame facedly away. No one went near the urinal, and they all hurried to bathe and dress and go on about their business of the day. Soon the head was empty and the naked guy lay alone, still in the urinal drain. His body quivered still with excitement, and his blood pounded when he remembered the row of grinning faces and gushing cocks crowded over him. Being all boots they had been boys in their late teens. Most naked or in scivvy shorts, and he thrilled to remember their trim, hard bodies, and full, hard cocks.

He lay in silence for a while, and then he heard the whistling of someone approaching. It was the orderly coming to clean the head. He scrubbed the bowls, and the basins, and whistled merrily while he worked. Finally he rounded the corner of the urinal. His mouth fell open and the mop fell from his hands. Slowly he read the sign and gazed at the man in the urinal. Moving closer he saw the man's body was covered with a juicy mixture of yellow and creamy light white liquids. A slow change came over his face and his eyes began to glow with sadistic delight.

Standing up again, he quickly stripped off all of his clothes and stood grinning with anticipation at the trembling man before him. His magnificent body aroused the man's passion and the two looked at each other while their cocks quickly rose to stiff throbbing positions. The orderly walked to the door and looked into the barracks. Satisfied that they were alone and would not be disturbed at this hour, he returned and stood over the man once more, enjoying thoroughly his mounting excitement and apprehension. Then with a short laugh he bent down and grasped the man by the hair. Roughly he dragged him out of the urinal and threw him full length out on his back on the floor. Kneeling beside him in the clear light, he reassured himself of the stuff smeared all over the man's body was what he thought it was, and with a short animal cry, he threw himself full length down on the bound and tied man.

In a frenzy of little groans and gasps, he writhed, rolled, and pressed his body on the man's slippery body. The full length of his body was soon smeared with the remainder of the morning's fantastic shower. He straightened up and drew his knees up to smear thoroughly his crotch and between his buttocks. He laid down again and stretched out his arms so that even his armpits were dripping with the seedy mixture. Grasping the man by the hair, he began to slide his body up and over the eager mouth, and every inch of his chest was crushed against the gasping lips, and the tongue lapped and reaped a rich harvest from the thick patch of matted hair in the middle of his chest which thinned out into small tufts around his full lush nipples. The hairy armpits were locked over the feverish mouth and licked clean. Slowly the rippling body moved up, giving the frantic tongue plenty of time to lick and suck each area carefully. An exciting line of hair led down from his chest to his navel, where it spread out in thick dripping matts covering his abdomen. The greedy, eager mouth lapped noisily over his forest of moist curly hair, but the long thick cock was denied him, and it slipped over his face as the hairy balls dropped into his mouth. Straightening up on his knees, the boy jerked the man's head roughly into his groin, thrilling to the feel of the hot tongue pushing hungrily into every crevice and corner. Sliding up, he brought his buttocks up around his face and crushed his asshole down around his mouth. A rough jerk that threatened to tear out his hair, sent the man's tongue pushing up against the hairy hole, and strained to force entry.

This exciting treatment had the boy moaning hysterically. Glancing back of him, he saw the man's cock standing up stiffly, jerking and glistening. Sliding back, he raised his buttocks up and maneuvered the head of it up against his asshole. Pushing down gently, he eased the hard cock slowly info his loins. Delirious at this new thrill, he began to raise and lower himself on his small trim buttocks, sliding the cock in and out of himself. The panting man underneath him began to arch his body upward to meet each downward thrust of the hysterical youth's. Soon a passionate sob broke from the man and he thrust his hips up in sharp thrusts that drove his cock deep into the boy's entrails. As he poured his lead out in rapid spurts, the sensation was more than the hysterical youth could stand. With a cry, he threw his whole body back to receive the full length of the gushing cock and grabbed his cock to train the full stream of his own spurting cream into the face of the man stretched before him. The violent throbbing of his asshole drained the man's last drops out in rapid spurts and finally his cock began to limp and dropped down on the panting abdomen before him.

After a few moments the boy regained his breath and untied the man's arms and legs. Jerking him to his feet, he grabbed him by the balls and pulled him roughly behind him into the shower room. Refreshed by the invigorating water, the youth renewed his assault and reduced the man to complete submission with only raw force. Five more times the youth proved his mastery of the man in violent struggles that rose each to convulsive orgasms in both of them. The master forcing his slave to submit to violent and degrading acts, letting his sadistic instincts run wild.

Finally after his rape-like assaults, the youth calmed down, dressed and went his way. The broken and bleeding man lay sobbing softly, once again tied up in the drain of the urinal, where the boy had first discovered him and had thrown him again when he had finished.

CHAPTER TWELVE
SALTY SHIPMATES

It was Saturday afternoon when the ship pulled into San Diego—and what a day that was for the crew! We had been out to sea for the past eight months on drills, and of course the married salts as well as the young single lads were hot to acquire a few drinks and a gal. Tijuana was the place that Claude and I decided on for a first liberty, and within two hours after docking we were in a cab whisking us toward some hot excitement in that amazing town.

The first thing we did was to hit one of the fancier clubs, and had not been stationed at the bar very long when a well-dressed man and woman bought us a drink. We thanked them and thought no more about it—but they continued buying and of course we were somewhat surprised and suspicious.

The lady was a redhead and very pretty. Her breasts were firm and round as well as her hips, and her waist was extremely small. She eyed both of us in a strange way...just as almost every "twat" we ever came in contact with did. I might say that Claude was absolutely with no exception the handsomest person I have ever seen. He was eighteen years old and had curly golden hair, with large brown eyes to set it off. His skin was deep bronze with six feet-one of body that was perfect in every respect; slim waist, firmly fleshed stern, stout neck and broad shoulders. Claude was an orphan and had always been on his own, so he knew plenty about life.

I happen to have the same kind of build, but my hair is raven black, with green eyes and a large mouth that many women have told me can put out some real sweet kisses and so forth. My body is about perfect also, but only because I have worked out with weights a lot—while Claude's is natural.

I'm a few years older than he, four to be exact, and naturally am the leader when we go out together.

"Boys, won't you join us at our table?" pleaded the redhead. I could tell she was highly interested in both of us. She's with some "gay guys" was the first thing that entered my mind, for both of us were constantly pestered to death by them! We only put out to a few to tell the truth. "Natch" we played with each other on board ship during cruises. I was librarian on our carrier. I had a bunk of my own and after closing the library I would let Claude slip in to spend the night with me. We would play phonograph records, cards, or each other!

Well, to save money, we accepted the redhead's invitation. She introduced herself as Betty Harrington and the handsome fellow with her as her husband. To our surprise there was no one else at their reserved table, and we were soon devouring a lavish dinner.

They were very interesting to talk to, and after we had consumed several more drinks, they both asked us how we would like to spend the weekend at their home in Beverly Hills. They knew their stuff, and by this time had sized us up as two square guys, which was correct.

It seems that they had a mansion with a large pool so we could lie around and relax and have about anything we would like. Naturally we accepted immediately, both expecting a "blow job" the moment we entered their big limousine. Strangely, nothing at all happened on the long drive.

We arrived at their home none the worse for wear, were given several more drinks, a light snack to eat, and were shown to our room for what was left of the night. It held the largest double beds I have ever seen, and I couldn't wait to get Claude in it beside me—this was real plush comfort. We slept in each other's arms and naturally didn't pass up this opportunity to rub each other off. We were too tired to try anything else!

Late the next morning, much to our delight, a maid brought us breakfast in bed. Later, a man servant appeared with swimming trunks and robes. Our hosts were nowhere in sight as we wandered about the huge house. At last we went out on the gorgeously landscaped grounds and found the swimming pool.

We played like eels in the clear tepid water for some time. We preferred to swim nude, and as no one appeared we took off our trunks. For a while we amused ourselves by trying to nip each other when we met underwater. Claude bit my love prong and wouldn't let go until I commenced to laugh and gag so hard that I practically drowned and he had to pull me to the surface.

Betty and her husband Ralph, as if by magic, were waiting for us at the edge of the pool, and we were both extremely embarrassed. They let on that they had not seen what had transpired!

We were entertained royally all day and neither of our hosts made any sign of taking advantage of us, much to our annoyance, for we both wanted desperately to get into Betty. They told us that a party was to be held that night, and that we were to be showed off in the best of style.

About six-thirty we went down to the great living room where Betty and Ralph were pouring drinks for a number of people. They were all quite young, the oldest being not more than twenty-five, and the youngest about eighteen. Later, more cars arrived, bringing both boys and girls. Drinks were given all of them as well as "weeds", much to my surprise.

After a slight begging on Betty's part, Claude and I smoked one too!

Around midnight, the party was at a frenzy pitch, and I commenced to get impatient—though not too much. There were several girls I was quite heated up about. I noticed couples were leaving the room, and after there were only five or six left, Betty came in and told us that the party was being continued downstairs in the trick room.

It was one of the most elaborate playrooms I had ever been in...and the people in it were doing the oddest things I had ever witnessed. Several of the girls and boys were tied up by their wrists with leather straps hanging from the wall, and they were being whipped.

"This is a meeting of our flagellation club," explained Betty. "Have you ever seen anything more devilish or exciting? We felt sure you boys would enjoy getting in on it."

Wild music was being played and several couples were dancing.

It was only a short time until many of the boys and girls were nude. They would kiss and lick each other and the boys would insert their weapons in any hole they could find. As the tempo of the party became faster, the play became rougher and tougher.

One handsome young man produced a rubber hose that was attached to a hot water faucet. Inserting it in a young tender girl, he turned it on. She screamed and lashed about while two strong youths grabbed her legs to keep her from pulling the hose out, while another put his tool in her behind.

The water ran in streams on the cement floor and another of the youths rolled in the water, barking like a dog!

Nearly an hour passed and I was becoming dazed by these mad activities. Then, before I knew what was happening, several strong lads grabbed both Claude and me, stripped us and tied us in a standing position facing each other so close we could feel the muscles of each other's stomachs. At least four of the young sadists started in doing what I will never forget—with their tongues.

One girl poured a bottle of champagne over our bodies. The others licked almost every inch of our bodies—the joy of it nearly drove us to distraction. Our legs were spread wide apart and we were kissed and fondled there until we were ready to burst with passion. I could not resist placing my tongue in Claude's mouth and we kissed rapturously, which greatly amused those watching us. Our organs had been rubbing against each other's belly for a while, but I managed to slip mine down and jammed it between his legs. Almost at once I reached a tremendous climax and spurted out a regular fountain of jizz. Some of our worshippers were so berserk with lust that they actually licked it off the cheeks of Claude's buttocks and his thighs as it streamed down!

One beautiful young girl now squeezed in between us and placed my still firmly erect organ in her slit; then she reached around and slipped Claude's in her back door! No sooner had this been accomplished than we were all three bound together in that position.

Betty came over and asked us if we minded. I told her, "No, no, NO! I'm having the most gawd awful good time I've ever had. Let's continue, before I lose my stiff!"

Some of them began lashing our bare buttocks. This would drive me forward against my companions, at each stinging blow, then an equally loud smack would send Claude forward, jamming the girl against my body. The hot fiery pain in my buttocks, mingling with the glorious thrilling sensation I was getting in front, sent the most unearthly shudders of ecstasy all through my body.

It was completely beyond anything I had ever experienced before or ever dreamed of. I must have discharged two or three times in the girl tied to me, and each time I could not help moaning with delight until I nearly fainted.

Our watchers must have decided that we were slowing up, for very shortly a young fellow was trying to stick his well-greased organ in my behind. Now this was nothing new, for Claude and I had tried it lots of times. However, this kid worked with such violence, his organ rubbing my old prostate gland, and slamming me forward against the girl, that it seemed a holocaust of fiery thrills had enveloped my loins. Another fellow was doing the same thing to Claude, forcing him forward, and the girl was wild with passion, was digging her teeth into my neck. It seemed that almost at the moment they were jammed against me forcing my organ into her to the limit, the fellow behind me would give a terrific shove crashing us together with a sensation like an exploding charge of T.N.T.!

I had thought that this was the ultimate, but I just didn't know from nothing. Before the performance was over, my buttocks had been warmed up plenty with a leather belt and three other fellows had driven their dongs into my behind. I got to the point where I felt like I was coming all the time! Nothing could be more incredible than that such emotion could be aroused in a man's body. At last we were untied and Claude and I sat down on a sofa to rest, not bothering to put on our clothes. We smoked another "weed" together, puffing on it by turns, and our two stiff bones never relaxed a bit. We were just too heated up.

There was one exceptionally gorgeous young man present, his body was perfect, the type you would suspicion God of spending just a little too much time on. His muscular legs were that deep brown of Southern California lads, and his organ reminded me of a third leg! This young fellow was higher than a kite from smoking weed, and would roll on the floor in what appeared to be agony, but seeing his facial expressions you could tell that he enjoyed it to no end. Shortly, two of the girls in the room produced some ping pong balls and commenced throwing them at this much heated up bundle of sex. As each ball struck his strong body he would shriek with joy, wiggling and turning, playing with himself all the while.

Betty told me to lay in his arms on the floor for a thrill I would never forget.

By that time, being in the kind of a heat to set the world on fire, I did. I lay on top of him and immediately he embraced my body with his arms, the strongest arms that ever encircled me. As each ball would come whizzing through the air at us, he would use me for a shield, rolling over on top of me, hiding his curly blond head under my arms and by these actions pressing close to my body.

His own body shook as though with a convulsion, and tears of happiness poured down his tanned face. I became so greatly aroused I thought for sure I would go raving mad. With all my strength I managed to roll him on the deck so that he was lying on his stomach. Grabbing my tool, I began pushing it slowly between the cheeks of one of the cutest, round and firmly plump pair of buttocks I have ever seen on a man. He was tight and began thrashing about and yelling because my organ was swelled up terribly large.

The youth tried his best to buck me off, but my teeth gripped his ear and he settled down fast.

After I had driven my shaft in up to the hilt, he didn't seem to mind so much. Slowly I pushed the throbbing implement in and out, building up to a glorious state of passion. Finally, with a grand spurt of action in moans of joy, I shot a huge load into him to the accompaniment of cheers from the watching guests. The spasms of intense pleasure shooting through me continued so long that I felt they would never cease.

Finally I got off my thoroughly exhausted stud. Claude got hold of me and told me to follow him into a small room nearby where he stated one of the strangest orgies was taking place. Of course, after the ping pong ball deal, nothing in the world would seem strange ever again.

Entering the room, I gasped in surprise. It was a huge marble shower room and in the center stood a beautiful girl circled by a number of the male celebrators. They were all aiming their tools at her and spurting urine over her nude body from head to toes, and she appeared to be enjoying this form of hot bath. One lad, stiff-legged, walked up to her magnificent love opening and while water was gushing from his powerful organ he inserted it.

A golden shower ran out of her slit and into a jeweled goblet held in the hands of another.

When it was full it was poured over her head and then the ceremony was repeated again! We stood watching these amazing antics, I with my arm about Claude's shoulders, and slowly my fires of lust mounted again.

"Please Claude," I begged him, "let me stick it into you once. I'm just crazy to shoot again!"

"Oh, you infernal bastard!" exclaimed Claude. "Lay down on the floor and I'll sit on top of you; I want to watch what goes on here."

Soon I was flat on my back, with my prong sticking up into

him and both my hands rubbing his big piece of meat until it throbbed. A girl entered the room with a goblet of red wine in her hand. Noticing us, she knelt down and pressed her lips to mine. Her arm was about Claude and the goblet of wine spilled down his back. It flowed between the crack of his buttocks and dripped over my balls. This created the most curious sensation and astonishingly enough, I reached another terrific climax. I squirmed so much that soon Claude had shot a big load of cream out over my belly.

Not long after this, dinner was served and everyone trooped upstairs to the dining room and crowded about a long table loaded with every imaginable delicacy—including many hot oily dishes so everyone could go home halfway in their senses.

Before the serving began, Betty inquired if the gathering would like a hormone martini. Apparently no one knew what kind of a drink that was, so Betty commenced to show us.

Grabbing one of the more bashful youths in the room who had only discharged once in that sinful evening, she latched onto his stick with both hands and soon beat him off into a large glass of martinis.

It reminded me of the foam on the head of a beer. Placing a few olives in the glass, she passed it around the room much to the excitement of all concerned.

Almost everyone tasted it, and the newness of this trick nearly put all of us into hysterics. I must admit that it didn't taste unusual. However, by that time probably anything would have tasted good. We continued eating and drinking martinis in this fashion for such a period of time that we completely ran out of the ingredients for making them! The poor youth gave up trying to produce more cream, and announced that he had better be getting home in time to catch the milk man!

Claude and I retired to our room more than exhausted, but after a shower we were refreshed and slept like two babies.

We did not wake up until mid-day and after breakfast-lunch went to the beach with Betty and Ralph. We had a lot of fun chasing around with them, but turned in early that night as we had to make it back to the base in the morning.

As we had suspected, Betty and Ralph slept with us and he let each of us take Betty on once and then he made her. He said he liked it better after we had warmed her up. She was one dame who certainly knew how to entertain a fellow! Also, we took turns pouring it to Ralph from behind while he was on top of Betty.

We had one hell of a time that night until all of us were played out.

CHAPTER THIRTEEN
TAKING A PISS

I had to take a hell of a piss, so I went into this garage and asked if I might use this toilet. The young mechanic said it was okay, but he was getting ready to close up and while I went into the can he started putting out lights around gas pumps. I was pissing away when this six foot four inch mechanic came in.

"There," he said. "Everything's locked up. Hey, how about sticking around for a few minutes? I gotta take a shit, and like someone to talk to while I'm shitting."

"Sure, I'm in no hurry," I said, and moved around where I could get a good view of him as he stepped into the open-fronted-cubicle. He started to take his pants down at once. He had black wavy hair, and all his exposed skin was dirty and greasy. When he dropped his pants, I saw he had on yellowed Jockey shorts which had holes in them, and they were stained with piss in the crotch. When he pulled the shorts down, I nearly passed out. He had a fat cock with bulging veins and it had fore-skin on it that hung an inch below the head. It must have been ten inches, soft. He sat down on the john and I noticed that his balls hung right into the water. By then I had a rampant hard-on and I suppose he noticed it. He grinned at me and said, "I got something for you. Something you're gonna like. Now get your clothes off. All of them."

It took me a few seconds to strip, and I dropped on my knees in front of him and started licking his boots. "Lay down on the floor, you bastard. That dried piss on the floor should taste good for you. Go at it."

I threw myself on the filthy floor and he stood up from the toilet and with his toe, rolled me over on my back. Pulling his shorts and pants off his legs, he squatted over my face with his ass right at my nose and farted. It was a really foul smell, and excited the hell out of me. As I stared up at his asshole, I saw it open and, slowly a big black turd came oozing out. I started jerking off as the shit came closer and closer to my lips. It was a real fat lump of shit and it was at least eight inches even before it was completely out of his dirty asshole.

I started sucking on the shit as it was coming out. Then I couldn't wait any longer and bit right into the shit, eating and licking it.

By this time the mechanic was all ready with a long, fat, swollen prick. He stood up quickly with shit still sticking from his asshole and stood over me watching me chew on his shit. The pecker had grown a good three inches and had an enormous red head on it. Before I knew it he was pissing all over me and I was drenched in his strong-smelling urine while still lapping up the last of his shit. He suddenly reached down and grasped my wrists in a piece of rope and jerked me to my feet. My arms were being tied to the pipe overhead. He pulled on his own shorts and pants and then went out of the can without an explanation.

I hung there stark naked, scared to death and completely helpless. In about five minutes he was back...with a *cop*.

The cop started to call me filthy names and was slapping my face. I could see he had a hard-on and a big one that reached nearly to the top of his high boots. Then they both stripped and the cop shoved his huge dong into my asshole without even spitting on it. As I screamed in pain, the mechanic pissed all over both of us. He shot a load into my ass that felt like a pint.

The cop then put me on my knees and forced me down with his long billy club running up my ass nearly to the handle. Then they both stood in front of me, hands on hips, bare-ass naked, and made me suck both of those shit-covered cocks that had just been up my sore asshole until they were clean.

Before finally letting me go, they both took my name, address and phone number. Now I know that they can come and make me go through that all over again anytime they want, and there is nothing I can do about it. It all happened only ten days ago and already both have been back with buddies of theirs. I told them they would have to give me a rest. My ass is so sore all the time I can hardly sit down, but they just slap my face and tell me they'll put me through my filthy paces whenever and wherever they want and that I have nothing to say about it and will probably like it. And I guess I do, kind of.

CHAPTER FOURTEEN
TORTURED WITH SEX

Ed was a tall guy—over six feet. He had a slender body covered lightly with hair which matched the dark, wavy hair of his attractive head. He was not a muscular guy, but certainly well-developed, and anyone who saw him desired to "have" him. I was one of these people. I not only wanted to get this guy to kneel down to me, but I wanted to exhibit him to my buddy, Pete. Ed and I went through the preliminaries and finally he agreed to go home with me for some good dirty sex. I could tell by talking to him that he was the "slave" type and would be willing to do the whole scene with anyone who needed a slave. I needed a slave damn bad—one who could and wanted to do anything and everything that entered my evil mind. I hadn't had a real good session with anyone on the rack for a hell of a long time, and I knew tonight would be the night, and Ed was my victim. Not only that, but I would have an accomplice—Pete would be even more willing than I am to test this guy's endurance and capacity.

On the way home I gently teased Ed with vague things of what would happen to him, and also found out some of the things he liked to do. When we reached the house, I led him in and locked the door behind us and we both knew that this would be a night to remember and there was no backing out for anyone now.

I shoved Ed into the room and he stumbled to the floor. I told him to stay there and that from this moment on, when either

Pete or I would say or even suggest anything, that he would be better off to do as we suggested or else he'd suffer. He knew I wasn't kidding so he stayed prone on the floor. Pete came out of the bedroom and I turned and said to Pete, "I've brought us a real prize, Pete; he's willing to take us both on and says he loves to be tortured and used anyway we can possibly think of. He says he's been a slave many times and never gets enough. Think we can give him enough?"

Pete grinned at me and then at the slave and said, "Hell, yes, this son of a bitch will wish he'd never set foot into this room when I'm through with him."

I cautioned Pete, "He doesn't go for any cutting or bruising—doesn't like to have his body marked in any way, and I told him we'd give our word. Of course, belt marks soon pass away, but we won't cut him or blister or bruise him." So we promised.

Now we began. I yanked the slave to his knees and told him to suck the crotch of my Levi's and kiss my clothes all over. Then I kicked him in the crotch and he fell on his back. Pete and I went over to him and began ripping and tearing his clothes from his body: prodding and punching and roughing him up. Finally he lay back completely nude and Pete and I stood back and admired our "slave". He was indeed sexy as hell, and he was well hung—big balls and nice cock. We told him to roll over on his stomach, and when he rolled over we both got excited at seeing his well-rounded and inviting hairy ass. Pete grabbed his belt and let the leather bite the cheeks of Ed's ass, and with each snap of the belt, the slave squirmed and slithered along the floor; I grabbed him and pulled him to his knees and told him to undress me with his mouth—not to use his hands, and if he did, Pete would whip him on the back. So he began to undress me, pulling with his teeth and unbuttoning one button at a time until my Levi's were open and he pulled them to the floor. He pulled my T-shirt over my head and that left me nude with my pants around my ankles on my boots. Pete knew he'd have to use his hands to get these off; and he posed ready with the belt, and when the slave had my pants off and was crying with pain from the leather belt, I made him suck my boots and kiss the leather, and suck and lick my legs all the way to my crotch. When his hot tongue reached my crotch, I grabbed his head, and with my one hand, held his head so he couldn't turn it, and with the other I took my "cheesy" and dripping, throbbing cock and rubbed it under his nose and made him lick it. After he had licked the head clean and had sucked the juice from the hole, I shoved it into his mouth and rammed it down his throat. I told Pete to hold his head, and then I fucked him hard—showing no mercy to him and just jammed it in and yanked it out until he began to gag and choke, and we let him fall to the floor exhausted and panting.

Pete came up to him and tied his arms and legs outstretched on the floor and stood over him and began to undress. With each piece Pete took off, he hit Ed with it and he threw his leather boots at Ed's cock and balls and then made Ed lick his feet and suck his toes. Our slave was helpless and was eager to do anything we asked so that he wouldn't be beaten.

I had to piss and so did Pete, so we decided to use our slave as a toilet. I stood over his body and began to let the piss trickle out on his head and nose and mouth. I told him to open his damn mouth and drink the piss and as his mouth filled with my piss the foam ran down his cheeks and neck between each swallow. Pete was behind me and pissed wildly all over the slave's body, concentrating on his cock and balls. We noticed as Pete's warm piss bathed the slave's cock, his cock began to get harder and harder, and began to throb from the excitement of two big guys standing over his helpless body with their big cocks and balls spraying piss all over him.

I turned to Pete and asked him if he thought that we should do something about that hard-on. Pete said hell yes, we should jack him off and make him eat his own come. The slave protested, saying he didn't want to come until the end because he always lost all desires after he came and he couldn't and didn't want to do anything after he came. So we laughed at him, telling him how helpless he was and that since he didn't want to come, that

that's just what he was going to do. I knelt down and started to play with his cock and sucked it hard. I put his balls in my mouth and yanked on them hard, pinching them between my teeth so that the slave squirmed and begged for mercy. Pete knelt over his head and shoved his nine inch cock into the slave's mouth so that he couldn't complain. This seemed to help. As long as we kept the slave busy sucking or kissing or licking our bodies, the other one could do just about anything to him. His mind was too busy sucking to think about the pain. Finally he was ready to come and I told Pete to sit on his mouth and make him suck his ass while he came, so Pete did. Finally the slave shot his load and I caught it in my hand. He jerked and squirmed and blew a big load and he tried to force his head away from Pete's ass, but Pete kept making him suck his asshole long after he came. We stood away from him and let him gasp and groan and then Pete let him up. I told the slave to come over and lap the juice out of my hand but he said he wouldn't. So Pete took the belt and began to whip him. The slave took as much as he could and finally crawled over and lapped the juice out of my hand. He took every drop of his come and swallowed it.

While he was kneeling on the floor I told him to suck my cock and to keep at it until we told him to stop. He went down on my throbbing dick as I watched Pete take the mint salve and begin to rub it on the slave's asshole. This salve was real hot and spicy, and it began to burn and itch the slave's hole like crazy. The hotter it stung and the more it itched, the faster he sucked. Finally the itching and burning became so severe that he tried to shove his finger up his hole to scratch it. Pete grabbed his hands and had him handcuffed to the chair, and then tied him over a stool and tied his legs to the stool so he couldn't move and his ass was exposed to our mercies. Pete kept rubbing more mint on his hole and finally he begged us to help the itching. So Pete got the rubber tube and gently inserted the tip into the slave's ass. He pulled it out and the slave begged for more. His ass was so hot that anything would help. So Pete bent down and posed the tube at the hole and then with a hard thrust sent the tube ramming in to the slave's ass. The slave groaned with pain and pleasure. Pete and I took turns ramming things up his ass and fucking him in the mouth, and once or twice Pete rammed his cock up the slave's ass, but he couldn't leave it there because the mint burned the head of his cock and he would pull out his cock and ram it into the slave's mouth to clean and cool it. The slave was really being tortured now; he had lost all desires to suck, but we forced him to suck our cocks and made him lick the mint and grease off the rubber tube. Pete said he was getting hot as hell and wanted to blow his load, so he shoved the tube up the slave's ass and taped his hole shut. Then he untied the slave and shoved him against the wall so he had to sit with the tube up his ass. Then Pete began to fuck the slave in the mouth and he told me to stand next to him and as he fucked the slave, I should piss on the slave's face and mouth so he would have to drink some of my piss while he was sucking Pete's cock. Pete finally shot his load and rammed his cock down the slave's throat while I pissed on Pete's balls and the crack of his ass, and on the slave's head.

When Pete was through and the slave had eaten all of Pete's come, he turned around and made the slave lick the piss off his ass and balls. While Pete was having his ass licked, I started to jack myself off. I told Pete to lie on the floor and let me come on his body.

Pete laid on the floor and knelt over him and made the slave jack me off on Pete's stomach and cock and balls. I had a big load and really covered Pete with my come. After I was through, I rubbed the slave's nose in my come and made him smell and eat some of it. Then I sat on Pete's belly and got my balls and ass all full of my come and made Ed lick it off. He knelt down and sucked my balls and my asshole clean while Pete was pulling the tape off his ass and the tube came slithering out.

Pete and I smoked cigarettes and thought of our next move. The slave lay there before us begging to be released. We told him we weren't through yet, and tied him flat to the floor, his body outstretched. Then we took clothespins and pinned them to his nipples and then pulled the pins off. When his nipples were red and big we each took a candle and lit it and let the wax drop on his tits. He groaned with agony but he couldn't move. When there was a good deposit of wax on each nipple we stuck the candles in upright and let them burn. Then we took two more candles and let the hot wax fall on his belly and cover his cock and balls. Then we took a rope and tied his balls and took the other end and put it through a pulley in the ceiling and took turns pulling on the rope. Each time we yanked it hard we made the slave squirm and jump so that more wax was spilled on his body. Finally we pulled the rope as tight as we could, which made the slave arch his body and the wax run over the candles. He cried with pain and so I stood over his face and pissed in his mouth whenever he opened it. Finally we pissed the candles out and let him up to remove the wax from his aching body. Then we tied a heavy weight to his balls and made him drag the weight behind him while he crawled on his knees from one side of the room to the other, sucking our cocks.

CHAPTER FIFTEEN
LEATHER FUN

The motorcycle race was over, and some of the racers were still in the locker room as I went in to see what I could see. There were only a few of them left, and Joe called me over as I came in.

"Hey," he said, "I'm going to ride my bike back home, and inasmuch as it's stripped for racing, would you mind taking my leathers with you in your car? I'll pick 'em up later this evening."

"Sure enough," I said, and my breath came a little faster as he tossed over to me his leather pants, his black leather shirt, his boots, his gloves, his helmet, goggles and all. As I gathered them into a convenient bundle for carrying, I noted that the leather had seen much use from his racing, that there was a delicious odor of oil, grease and sweat to them, and I wrapped them in a bundle. "Pick 'em up tonight?" I asked him, trying to keep a casualness in my voice.

"Sure enough," he replied, "sometime after supper."

"Good enough," I answered, and I left the locker room with this most delightful bundle of heavenly leathers under my arm.

A short time later back in my apartment, I opened the bundle of leathers and laid them out on the bed. *Why not?* I thought. *He won't be here for hours, and I can enjoy them until he gets here.*

Quickly shedding my own clothes, I pulled on his leather pants and buttoned them around my waist. They were just one size or two too small, and they confined my legs, calves, and buttocks and hips with a wonderful feeling of greasy leathery confinement. His recent addition of oil, grease, and sweat made the leather cling tightly to my skin, and my cock stiffened almost immediately. Next was the black leather shirt, quite well worn, slightly sweaty and smelling of oil and old leather, and it, too, being slightly small for me confined my upper torso in a most appealing way. The boots were rather old, loaded with grease, oil and track dirt, and they almost became a part of my skin as I slipped them on over the tight fitting pants legs. The helmet and goggles seemed to be made for my head, and in a pocket I discovered a black leather face mask. I adjusted the mask over my face, and it confined my nose, mouth, cheeks, ears and around my eyes in its delightful leathery embrace, covering my entire face with a piece of black supple leather which caused my heart to beat in double-time. The black leather gloves and large cuffs on them which came part way up my arms, held the leather sleeves of the shirt tightly in place against my flesh.

I moved over in front of a rather large full length mirror I had previously installed, and, through the eyeholes of the black leather mask around my face, I inspected the image that presented itself therein. As I viewed myself in the mirror, I saw a black leather clad man, now looking very similar to those many other racers who had been at the track all day, keeping me in a perpetual state of exciting hard-ons. I pulled the goggles down over my eyes to cover the eyeholes of the mask. Previously, looking at myself with my naked eyes, had caused a wonderful sensation to flow through my body, but the blue lenses of the goggles intensified the blackness of the leathers I was wearing, and my heart gave a double jump, my breath became faster, and my cock renewed its hardness at this newly darkened, intriguing spectacle.

I felt that I was just about ready for anything which might present itself from any willing fellow who might present himself, and was becoming momentarily more excited when in the next moment I was startled to hear a voice which broke in upon my wonderful reverie by saying, "What the hell's going on here?" I wheeled around and there was Joe standing just inside the door. In my eagerness I must not have locked the door, which he proceeded to do, and then coming over to me he said, "The last guy who donned my leathers without my permission had to pay for it...but good."

"What do you mean?" I stammered, and then said, "If you object, Joe, I'll take everything off right now," and I started to pull off one glove.

"No, never mind," Joe said, "if you feel so much like wearing my leathers, I'll fix it so you can really enjoy them, okay?"

"I was just trying 'em on Joe," I said.

"I'll fall in with that," he said, and then indicating my bed, he said, "here, lie down on the bed there."

I began wondering what he would do. It wasn't very long until I found out. He pulled some long strings of rawhide leather from out of his pocket and in a few moments he had me tied securely to the bed with my arms and legs spread-eagled, and tied securely to the four corners of the bed. I flexed my arms and legs and found that these knots were good, and immediately knew that I couldn't get away from that position if I had wanted to, but that he or someone else would have to untie me.

"Just so you won't make too much noise and wake the neighbors," he said with a grin, and he took a wide piece of soft black leather out of his coat pocket, partly removed the mask I was wearing, and in a second he had wrapped the leather around my mouth, chin and back of my neck effectively gagging me. Quickly, he replaced the leather mask, and it, too, helped to hold the soft leather underneath in place.

I had willingly let myself get into a position where I was securely tied on the bed, completely covered with black leather, and was now gagged with leather. For a moment I felt panic as I thought, "Now, I am at this guy's complete mercy for whatever he may decide to do." It wasn't long before I found out. His confining, tight-fitting leather all over my body and the soft leather gag on my mouth, plus the complete helplessness into which I had let myself be placed, were all having their effect on me, and I could feel my cock pushing out from beneath the tight-fitting, oily, greasy, leather pants.

"You wanted to wear my leathers," said Joe, "so you're going to wear 'em all night, and just like that, my friend."

He went to the phone and dialed a number. He spoke into the phone, "Pete? This is Joe. Hop on your bike and come over here to this place, yeah, the apartment I told you about. I got him all fixed up for you, and I think you'd like to take a crack at him. He had all my leathers on like I thought he would when I came in. Better wear your leathers, too."

He hung up the receiver, and looked my way with a grin. "Man, you're in for it, but plenty." I tried to make a sound, but only a faint noise came from under the leather gag which Joe apparently didn't hear.

It seemed only a few minutes until a faint knock came on the door, and Joe went to the door, unlocked it, and then it stood open. Pete stood just outside the door, and he immediately came into the room and stood there as Joe locked the door behind him.

I could see he was tall with broad shoulders and hips, with long, fine legs, well-muscled and taut. He wore heavy, stiff black leather boots which curved to his calves and pressed tightly to his knees. Black leather breeches covered his thighs tightly and flared and came back to cover snugly over his waist. The outline of a huge, throbbing cock made a little spot on the leather. He wore a black leather shirt and over that, a tight-fitting jacket of black leather. He wore a helmet of black leather and on his hands heavy gloves of leather with hard stiff cuffs that extended to his elbows.

Over his face, a black leather mask of tight, glistening leather outlined the square contour of his jaw, his high, wide cheek-bones. He wore goggles with dark lenses, and from behind I could make out the steady intent passion in his eyes.

An odor of gasoline and leather filled the room. My heart throbbed and beat, and my cock trembled wildly in my leather pants. Pete's black leather outfit glistened.

"God, what a beautiful setup," I heard him half whisper

through his black leather mask.

"He's all yours, Pete," Joe said, indicating me on the bed. "I'm going out for an hour or so, have fun." Joe unlocked the door, let himself out, and I heard the key in the outside lock relocking it. Pete moved to the side of the bed with the grace of a panther.

He stretched himself down on the bed next to me, and he rubbed his leather-covered cheek against mine, and I soon felt his strong, leather-covered arm around me. In a moment he caressed the leather pants I wore, and, within the confines of the thongs restraining me, I moved my pelvis and abdomen against Pete's leather breeches. Pete held me harder and harder to him, and we rubbed our cocks together through the leathers, chest against chest, shoulder against shoulder, black leather-covered cheek against soft leather, and the feeling of beating ecstasy was ours.

With a mad holding together, Pete lay on me entwining his legs with mine, leather boot rubbing on leather boot, leather legs in leather legs, Pete lowered himself on the bed and rubbed his leather-covered face over my boots, on and up and around and up high on my legs. His hands rubbed my tight black legs, slipping softly toward my cock. With renewed effort Pete moved himself upward until the region of my mouth and nose were in his leather-covered crotch, and his arms stroked up and down on my black leathered, black booted legs. There we were: two men completely covered with black leather from head to foot, together in sex, the current of love and our friendship there, present in the great passions of the moment.

The odor of leather in his lungs, the feel of his leather boots and breeches rubbing on my leather boots and pants, the warm sliding of leather on leather, made Pete mad with desire. He unzipped my fly and released my imprisoned cock, now huge and throbbing, mad with desire. He began to stroke the head of it with his gauntlet, and his other hand was on my boots as he gently ran his hand up and down my leg, feeling the caress of leather on leather, feeling the excitement of another all in black at his side.

Pete continued to stroke my cock, and his hand was warm on the leather. Then he held it against his face, feeling the movement of the great cock on the leather of his cheek. And he began to massage it, leather rubbing smoothly over the tip of the cock. He took my balls in his hand and squeezed them gently. Then he began to massage them in his leather-gloved hand. His other hand was rubbing over and over on the head of my hot, stiff prick.

In a few moments I noticed and felt a few drops of clear, white fluid appearing at the head of my stiff joy stick, and Pete saw it at the same time. He unsnapped the mouthpiece of his leather mask and then quickly licked this fluid off with his tongue. This seemed to lend him extra excitement, and once his lips touched my hot, straining cock he seemed to go slightly berserk. His mouth slid down until the entire organ was within his cheeks, his tongue was whirling and licking the length of my tool as he raised and lowered his head, and once again I relived the thrills of having my organ in another man's mouth. I could hardly wait and my hips rose and fell, meeting his mouth, sending my tool down his throat deeper and deeper until with an all-embracing, agonizing joy and body-shaking shudder of sheer delight, I pumped a flow of syrup into his waiting and receptive mouth. He received it as I produced it—and I thought I would faint dead away as his mouth sucked vigorously for more. The gag around my mouth muffled my sounds, and this prevented him from accurately judging my feeling as he sucked and swallowed on my softening tool. When he finally realized the situation, he licked the last drop from my falling weapon, rose up from the bed, and went over to the mirror as he lighted a cigarette. He stood there admiring his own image as the clouds of smoke whirled above his leathered body and head.

I shut my eyes and seemed to pass out for a few moments, living in a world of utter enjoyment and unholy gleeful ecstasy.

A few minutes later Pete returned and lay alongside of me, and again our two black-leathered bodies were close together.

His booted legs surrounded mine, and his leather arms were around my tightly leathered body. Pete lay his cheek next to mine in a kiss of black leather. He began to move gently against me. He pushed his cock through my leather-panted legs and my cock lay against the smooth, soft, black leather of his breeches. Pete began to move faster and faster, pushing his cock against my leather pants, with his arms around me in an embrace of black-leathered passion. The leather on our bodies filled the air with the scent of excited sex.

Neither of us knew what was actually happening; we had both entered the semi-coma of exquisite, ecstatic passion where the only things in existence were each other, the tight, hard, shining black leather, and the feeling of the two of us close together in eternal embrace with our cocks throbbing and beating on the shining black leather.

Then in a convulsion of rapture, Pete hugged me closer, then tighter and tighter and hard in his black leather, and he pressed his arms around me; we kissed madly through the leather, and, rubbing our cocks even faster on the leather the agonies of ecstasy were more thrilling and throbbing, and we came, Pete into my leathers, and I again on Pete's tight leathered legs. Pressing our boots together, locked two as one, coming and coming, gism from two long stiff pricks wetting the leather, glistening on it, as we came again and again in an unending passion of joy and desire for each other and for black leather all around us, soft and hard and shining and tight black leather, and as we came, we came wet on the bed, desiring to be in each other's embrace for always.

CONCLUSION

There are those who will find these stories offensive. Some will describe them as obscene. But it is at least fortunate that we have made some advance against the machinery of censorship. True, a loud voice alone will not end the problem, but many intelligent voices can serve to plant the seeds of thought in other minds. This is not a small accomplishment. In the long run, perhaps it is the best way for an individual to "take arms against a sea of troubles."

One can understand that some persons of very modest character might object to certain materials—photographs of nude persons, or words descriptive of sexual properties and acts.

Probably the strongest objection to freedom of the press is the danger it presents to youth. In itself this argument strikes one as foolish, nor do the arguments offered in its support improve the matter. There is a lengthy fable, scarcely bearing repetition, of the young boy who orders a packet of seeds from a mail order firm and finds himself deluged with pornographic mailings. But assuming this could happen, we are left with a basic assumption that exposure to photographs or ribald stories will somehow miraculously convert our young man into a depraved creature of some unspecified sort.

There are families who raise their children in nudist surroundings. And if we overlook these children, who seem no better and no worse than their neighbors, and turn to the average individual, we would be hard pressed to find a single man or woman who did not, when young, encounter "dirty" words, in conversation, or scrawled on alley fences. Surely all of us have listened to a ribald story or two? French postcards and genuinely erotic photographs have never been too rare. No generation of monsters has been created. Surely today's young people are as able to cope with these matters as their parents and grandparents were? Might they not, indeed, be better equipped?

Then there are those who quickly point out that in the past we spoke of such things in whispers, accompanied by titters and giggles, and that such photos, like these Tijuana Bibles, were sold "under the counter." Well, a look at our divorce statistics, or figures on impotence in men, frigidity in women, and such, won't exactly convince us of the wisdom of that policy.

In the final analysis, we inevitably return to our consideration, that of whether man and his functions are or are not obscene. Has the individual man the right—perhaps even an obligation—to study himself and his functions, through whatever means?

If the answer to such a question is yes—and surely it must be if we are to cling to the ideals of our society—then man is not obscene; his actions are not obscene; his body is not obscene; and material such as the stories in this volume cannot be obscene because they deal with man and his actions—with a very real and very important aspect of his life. We cannot limit ourselves in this search for knowledge and appreciation. There is certainly no logic in saying, "I love my fellow man, I love everything about him—except for his genitalia, that is."

Of course, some may conclude that man is, after all, obscene. This being the case, there is little we can hope to do about the matter. We cannot even pray to our God—since he too must be obscene, and we have been created in his obscene image.

ABOUT THE AUTHOR

V. J. Banis is the critically acclaimed author ("the master's touch in storytelling..."—*Publishers Weekly*) of more than 200 published books and numerous short stories in a career spanning nearly a half century. A native of Ohio and a longtime Californian, he lives and writes now in West Virginia's beautiful Blue Ridge.

You can visit him at http://www.vjbanis.com

www.ingramcontent.com/pod-product-compliance
Lightning Source LLC
Chambersburg PA
CBHW050729250626
47155CB00005B/1718